Tweenie Genie

Tweenie Genie: Genie High School
first published in 2010
this edition published in 2012 by
Hardie Grant Egmont
Ground Floor, Building 1. 658 Chruch Street
Richmond, Victoria 3121, Australia
www.hardiegrantegmont.com.au

A CiP record for this title is available from the National Library of Australia

Text copyright © 2010 Meredith Badger
Illustration and design copyright © 2010 Hardie Grant Egmont

Cover design by illustration by Michelle Mackintosh
Text design by Sonia Dixon

Printed in China

1 3 5 7 9 10 8 6 4 2

Tweenie Genie

Genie High School

by
Meredith Badger

Illustrated by
Michelle Mackintosh

hardie grant EGMONT

Chapter 1

Which sort of school would you rather attend?

A: One where you learn algebra, or

B: One where you learn levitation?

If you're anything like Poppy Miller, you'd pick B, right? And like Poppy, you'd probably rather learn how to fly a magic carpet than learn to spell 'fluorescent', or say 'the dog is on the table' in German.

But here's one major difference between you and Poppy Miller. Poppy is a genie, and

you ... well, I'm guessing you're probably not. This means you have no choice but to go to a normal school, or 'normie' school as genies call it. But Poppy is a tweenie genie, which means she's supposed to go to a genie high school.

Did you notice we said *supposed* to go? That's because even though Poppy passed her Stage One genie training *two weeks* ago, she still hadn't started Stage Two at Genie High. She had to wait, and the time was going very slowly. Genies aren't known for their patience at the best of times, and when they're waiting for something really exciting to start, it drives them crazy!

All Poppy knew was that she'd soon be summoned to start the second part of her training. But she had no idea when or even *how* this summoning would occur.

hot temper

high ponytail

can touch her nose with her tongue

bangle

hates crusts

good at hiding in small places

Introducing Poppy

This is why when the doorbell rang during breakfast one morning, Poppy's heart immediately leapt into her mouth. Was this what she'd been waiting for?

Poppy wanted to race to the door straight away. But she knew she had to stay calm, because she didn't want to make her family suspicious. You see, no-one in Poppy's family knew that she was really a genie. Not her mum, not her dad and *definitely* not her older sister Astrid.

In fact, until recently, Poppy herself hadn't known anything about her genie-ness. She'd always considered herself to be the most normal, ordinary girl around. She had nice (but normal) straight brown hair and nice (but ordinary) brown eyes. She wasn't tall, but she wasn't short. She wasn't top of her

4

class, but she wasn't at the bottom either. The only thing that was at all unusual about Poppy Miller was that she could squeeze into small spaces and touch her nose with her tongue.

See what we're getting at? Poppy was average. *Totally* average.

So when a genie appeared on her twelfth birthday and told Poppy that she had something called the 'Genie Gene'... well, let's just say it wasn't until Poppy found herself actually *inside* her very own genie bottle that she believed any of it was true.

The morning the doorbell rang seemed like any other morning in the Miller household. The only thing slightly different was that Poppy's dad was away on a work trip, so her mum was

rushing around even more frantically than usual. Astrid was bragging about how she'd topped her class in a recent test, and Poppy was staring at her crusts, wondering how she could possibly get out of eating them. (Like all genies, Poppy hated crusts.)

When the doorbell rang, everyone stared at each other. 'Who on earth could that be?' said Poppy's mum.

'I'll go and check,' said Poppy, jumping up. She sneaked a couple of crusts into her pocket and deposited them in the pot plant near the front door. Her heart was pounding loudly as she turned the doorhandle. Who would be behind it?

But when the door swung back, there was no-one there at all. *Oh,* thought Poppy, horribly disappointed.

Then she spotted a star-speckled envelope on the front doormat, addressed to her mum and dad. Poppy picked it up, noticing with a little thrill how the address seemed to shimmer and glitter in the sunlight.

That's genie ink, realised Poppy as she hurried back to the kitchen.

DID YOU KNOW?

A letter written with genie ink will change depending on the reader. If the reader is a normie, the letter will match how well they can read. When a genie reads it, they see special words written between the normie lines.

'It's a letter,' Poppy said, handing it to her mother as casually as she could.

Her mum put it down and kept rushing around. 'Thanks, Poppy. I'll open it later.'

Poppy frowned. She didn't want to wait!

Luckily, Astrid was just as curious as Poppy. 'Open it now, Mum,' she begged. 'It's probably about something I've won.'

Poppy rolled her eyes. But annoying as Astrid was, her request did the trick.

'All right, then,' smiled their mum, reaching for the letter. But as she read, her smile faded and was replaced by a look of astonishment.

'What does it say?' asked Astrid, almost falling off her seat with impatience.

Mrs Miller laid the letter down on the kitchen table. 'I think,' she said, 'you should read it for yourselves.'

Astrid snatched the letter up and read it out loud.

8

Dear Mr and Mrs Miller,

We are delighted to inform you that your daughter, Poppy, has been accepted into the prestigious School for Incredibly Gifted Students on a full scholarship.

This may come as a surprise, given Poppy's less than remarkable school record, but at our school we believe that the most 'gifted' student is not necessarily the one who has won the most awards.

We'd like Poppy to start with us straight away. One of our senior teachers will arrive at your house shortly to greet you and take Poppy to her first day of school.

Yours truly,

Lady Topaz

Principal

Astrid slammed the letter down. 'Part of this letter is missing,' she declared. 'The part where it says it's all a big fat joke.'

Poppy examined the letter and smiled. Astrid was almost right. Only part of the letter was visible to normie eyes. But Poppy, with her special genie vision, was able to read the secret lines written between the other ones.

Good news, Poppy!
Genie High School starts today. Because there is so much to learn, you will no longer be attending night classes as well as going to normie school like you did during Stage One. Instead, you will attend Genie High full-time. Obviously, your family mustn't know what's going on. I'll be arriving soon to pick you up!
Lexie X

A warm glow washed over Poppy when she saw the signature. Lexie had been her Stage One genie trainer. She also happened to be a member of the Genie Royal Family and was known to most genies as Princess Alexandria. But to Poppy, she would always just be Lexie.

Poppy's mum leant over and hugged her. 'Sweetheart,' she said. 'I'm so proud!'

'Umm, thanks,' said Poppy, feeling a little embarrassed. She couldn't quite believe her mum had fallen for the letter.

Astrid, however, was not so convinced. 'It's just a stupid trick,' she kept muttering. 'It *has* to be.'

Just then, the doorbell rang again. 'I'll get it!' Poppy practically sang.

Standing on the front doorstep was a kind-looking and also very ordinary-looking lady.

11

But Poppy noticed something familiar about those deep green eyes. And wasn't her ponytail a little too high for an ordinary person?

'Lexie?' whispered Poppy.

Lexie winked. 'Just let me do the talking,' she instructed quietly. 'I've brought something that will help us gloss over any problems.'

'Who is it, love?' asked Poppy's mum, appearing in the doorway.

'Good morning, Mrs Miller. I am a teacher from Poppy's new school,' said Lexie, shaking hands. 'You must be so proud of your clever daughter.'

'She has *two* daughters,' said Astrid, joining the group. 'One of them has a whole shelf full of trophies, while the other has none.'

'Our school is perfectly equipped to bring out your daughter's true potential,' Lexie said,

ignoring Astrid. 'And we'd like her to start straight away. She can come with me now.'

'I'll come too,' said Mrs Miller. 'I'm dying to see the school.'

Poppy froze. If her mum came along, she'd guess straight away that the scholarship was not to any ordinary school! But Lexie didn't seem at all concerned. She pulled out what looked like a tub of lip balm from her bag and dabbed some shimmering gloss onto her lips.

'That's really not necessary, Mrs Miller,' she said, with a dazzling smile. 'You've already seen it, remember?'

As Lexie spoke, the minty smell of the lip gloss filled the air, and a vague expression came over Mrs Miller's face. 'Oh, yes,' she said. 'I just forgot.'

'I thought so,' smiled Lexie. Then she put her hand on Poppy's shoulder. 'Come along, dear. We've a busy day ahead of us.'

Poppy nodded. 'See you, Mum,' she said, kissing her still-dazzled mother goodbye.

Astrid scowled. 'There's been a mistake,' she insisted. 'A massive one.'

'No mistake,' said Lexie firmly. 'Hurry up, Poppy. We don't want to be late.'

'See ya, Astrid,' Poppy said, blowing a cheeky kiss to her sister. 'Have fun at school!'

Chapter 2

Lexie led Poppy briskly out the front gate. Then, the moment they were out of sight of the house, Lexie turned to her and said, 'Is your bedroom window open?'

'I think so,' replied Poppy. 'Why?'

'Because we need to sneak back in there and get your things for Genie High,' Lexie said with a grin.

'But my room is upstairs,' Poppy pointed out.

Lexie opened her eyes wide. 'Poppy Miller! Have you forgotten how to levitate?'

Poppy blushed. 'No,' she said. 'I just forgot that I *could!*'

Lexie and Poppy sneaked around through the back gate of the house and crept up until they were right underneath Poppy's window. Then they sat down cross-legged.

Poppy relaxed and closed her eyes. She had found levitation very difficult at first, but now she knew how to keep her mind empty of all thoughts except those that would help her float upwards. Today she thought about seagulls with kites attached to their wings. Sure enough, she soon felt the strange rising feeling in her tummy that meant she was floating upwards.

'That's enough, Poppy!' Lexie whispered.

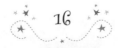

She suddenly sounded far away.

Poppy opened her eyes to find herself hovering in front of her bedroom window. She grinned. Even though she was used to levitation now, it was still a thrill. And it was great fun floating into her bedroom through the window. Poppy really hoped her mum wouldn't choose that moment to walk into her room. She would certainly get a big shock if she did!

Lexie floated in behind her a moment later. Then she pulled something out of her bag and handed it to Poppy. 'Here's your Genie High uniform,' she said.

Poppy looked at it, surprised. It looked – well, it looked like a *normie* school uniform. 'Are you sure this is right?' she asked doubtfully. 'I want to look like the other students.'

Lexie smiled. 'Trust me, OK?' she said. 'Now, get changed and gather up the rest of your things.'

Once Poppy had the uniform on, she grabbed her red tweenie backpack and her Location Lamp.

Location Lamps are how genies travel from one bottle to another. You see, genie bottles aren't all gathered in one place. They're scattered throughout the normie world, hidden

in the back of cupboards and the darkest corners of garden sheds. You might even have a genie bottle or two in your own house.

genie bottles come in all shapes and sizes

hidden in a junk shop in Newcastle

hidden in a restaurant in Frankfurt

hidden in a shed in Melbourne

hidden in the basement of some flats in Brooklyn

Genie bottles

Poppy's mind whirled with excitement. She had so many questions. What would Genie High be like? How many new tweenies would there be, and would she know any of them? Poppy had done her Stage One training with a group of tweenies – Rose, Hazel and Jake. She hoped they'd be there too.

But right then, there was no time to ask questions. Poppy knew her mum might walk in at any minute. 'OK, I'm ready,' Poppy announced, a little breathlessly.

Lexie looked at her with one eyebrow raised. 'Are you sure you haven't forgotten something?' she asked, a small smile at the corner of her mouth.

Poppy looked around. 'I don't think so ...'

Then one of the tassels from the old rug she was standing on brushed against her

ankle. To anyone else, it might've looked like it had been blown by a breeze from the open window. But Poppy knew better. She bent down and scooped the rug up. 'Sorry, Rocket,' she said. 'I didn't mean to forget you!'

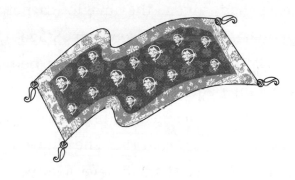

The carpet waved one of its corners in a way that couldn't possibly have been caused by the wind.

'His name is *Rocket?*' chuckled Lexie.

Poppy grinned. 'Well, he's almost like a pet to me,' she explained as she carefully

folded up the carpet and put it in her bag, 'so he needed a name. And he's very fast.'

Lexie nodded. 'I understand,' she said. 'Don't forget he used to be *my* carpet. I called him Speedster, but Rocket suits him better.'

Lexie had given the magic carpet to Poppy when she'd passed her Stage One training. It was kind of a gift for being a Golden genie. Poppy knew being Golden was a great honour, but she wasn't really sure what it meant. Lexie had said that she showed lots of promise – more than the average tweenie. But Poppy felt so normal! Still, she loved having a magic carpet of her own. And she couldn't wait to get to Genie High so she could ride it around at top speed and learn stunts.

'Let's get going now,' said Lexie. 'Where's your genie bottle?'

22

'It's under my bed,' said Poppy, crouching down to reach it. She knew it was very important to hide your genie bottle so that a normie didn't accidentally find it. Poppy felt around under the bed until her hand found something smooth and cold. Even in the gloom she could see the green glass of her genie bottle shining mysteriously.

Poppy unplugged the stopper and the faint smell of cinnamon wafted from it. She shivered with excitement. Finally, she was about to start Genie High!

Lexie linked her arm through Poppy's. 'Ready?'

Poppy nodded, and positioned one foot over the opening of the genie bottle. 'Definitely.'

The trick to squeezing into a genie bottle is to imagine yourself turning into something that can be poured – like water or sand – in through the bottle's narrow opening. Of course, you have to be a genie, too. The first time Poppy did it, it had felt very strange – like she'd been drinking lemonade while going down a swirly slide. The worst bit was when the journey ended and she fell over.

But I'm more experienced now, she reminded herself. She'd been in and out of her genie bottle every day while she'd waited to start Genie High School, and most of the time she landed on her feet.

Poppy closed her eyes and thought watery thoughts. As she started to flow into the bottle, everything started spinning and the floor dropped away. Then Poppy began

whooshing through the darkness – up, down, even sideways.

Suddenly the whooshing stopped and Poppy landed. Flat on her face!

'Nice landing, Teeny Weeny,' said a familiar voice. 'It's good to see that being a Golden genie hasn't changed you!'

Poppy half-groaned, half-laughed. She sat up and saw a boy her age standing there grinning. 'Hi, Jake,' she said. She was really glad to see him, although she wouldn't tell him that. Jake was quite confident enough already! 'What are you doing in my genie bottle?'

'I asked him to meet us here,' said Lexie, appearing beside her. Lexie's 'teacher' disguise had disappeared and she was now dressed in her usual funky genie clothes. 'I thought it'd

25

Lexie

be nice if we went to Genie High together.'

Poppy looked around excitedly. 'Are Rose and Hazel here too?' she asked. She was dying to see her other tweenie friends.

'I'm sorry, Poppy,' said Lexie, shaking her head. 'Rose and Hazel are going to a different school to you and Jake. Stage One tweenie classes are always split up to make sure you meet new people. But you can catch up with

them outside of school, of course.'

'Oh,' said Poppy, disappointed. She'd been looking forward to starting Genie High with *all* her friends.

'Don't worry, Teeny,' said Jake. 'You've got me at least. And once everyone knows that you're a Golden genie, you'll be the most popular student in the school.'

Poppy's tummy did a strange flip. She hadn't thought about everyone knowing. 'Um, Jake?' she said, biting her lip. 'Can you not tell everyone about the Golden stuff? I don't want to everyone to treat me differently.'

'But that's so boring,' Jake complained. 'You should be proud of being Golden.'

'I *am* proud,' said Poppy. 'It's just ...' It was hard to explain. *I'm just so used to being normal*, she thought. And the idea of everyone

treating her like she was 'special' made her feel weird.

'So, do you two want to stand around here and chat, or would you like to see Genie High?' said Lexie, raising an eyebrow.

'I'm ready!' said Poppy quickly.

'Me too!' said Jake.

Lexie smiled. 'I thought you might be. Then it's time for me to give you these.' She handed them each a sleek, silver gadget.

'Is it a mobile phone?' asked Poppy. Even Astrid didn't have one of those yet!

'No, it's a Dial-Up Device,' Lexie explained. 'You'll use it to find your way around Genie High.' She turned on the device and showed them a screen with a long list on it – Ruby Bottle, Sapphire Bottle, Tuckshop Bottle, Turquoise Bottle. 'These bottles are all part of

your school. You just find the place you need to go in the menu and click "send". The Dial-Up will take you there automatically. And you'll find it much more comfortable than using the Location Lamp, Poppy,' she added.

Poppy grinned. 'Thank goodness for that!'

'The Dial-Up has lots of other functions too,' said Lexie, 'but you'll discover those as you go along.'

'Excuse me, Oh Most Wondrous Tweenie,' said a small voice.

Poppy looked around. 'Who said that?' she asked.

'Your Dial-Up Device,' explained Lexie, laughing. 'It's set to the "ultra-polite" voice profile.'

Poppy picked up her Dial-Up. A small, friendly digital face had appeared on the

voice profile button: press to choose a personality for your Dial-Up (cheeky, super-strict, bossy, confused, ultra-polite, nagging, shy, grumpy, incredibly helpful, annoying)

mute button

send button: press this to go from one bottle to the next

bottle menu button: lists all the official Genie High bottles

class menu button: press to see all classes at Genie High

Dial-Up Device

screen. 'Hi,' she said, feeling quite odd talking *to* a phone rather than *into* one. 'Er, what's up?'

'I don't mean to interrupt as I know you're *really* busy,' said the Dial-Up, 'but you're due at the Genie High Entrance Bottle in one minute. If that's OK.'

'Same goes for you, boofhead,' chipped in Jake's Dial-Up. 'And how about brushing your hair for once?'

Jake frowned. 'What voice profile is *that*?'

'Cheeky, I'd say,' said Lexie. 'You can change it later, but now it's time to go. Press send at the top right of the screen. It'll take you straight to the Entrance Bottle.'

Poppy pressed the button and squeezed her eyes shut. Next stop, Genie High!

Chapter 3

Poppy was used to seeing amazing things since she'd become a genie. She'd visited genie shopping bazaars that were filled with weird and wonderful things, and she wouldn't even blink if someone flew around on a carpet or disappeared into a puff of smoke right before her eyes.

But when Poppy stepped into Genie High School for the first time, it took her breath away.

She was standing in a huge, orangey-yellow genie bottle with a long, twisted neck. The air was filled with unusual, but not unpleasant, smells – like fruits and flowers that Poppy couldn't identify. The most overwhelming thing about the place was the noise and the bustle. It was filled with young genies in school uniform, laughing and talking at the tops of their voices. They all seemed to be in a hurry and looked like they knew exactly where to go.

Everyone looks so grown-up, thought Poppy, suddenly feeling shy.

'Are we the only new ones?' asked Jake.

Lexie shook her head. 'There are some other brand-new Twos just over there.'

Poppy looked and saw a group of tweenies standing nearby. They were gazing around

with the same overwhelmed expressions that she and Jake had.

'How come they're wearing proper genie clothes?' Poppy asked, and glanced down at her normie outfit. Except it had somehow been replaced by the same uniform that the other tweenies were wearing. 'Hey!' she exclaimed. 'How did that happen?'

'Your uniform is made from chameleon fabric,' Lexie explained. 'It automatically adjusts to whatever situation you're in.'

'So when we go back to the normie world we'll look like we're wearing normie clothes?' asked Poppy.

Lexie nodded. 'Exactly.'

'Does it turn into pyjamas too?' asked Jake. 'That'd be great. I'll never have to get changed again!'

chameleon fabric saves genies having to change when they swap between the genie world and the normie world

adjusts to suit any situation in seconds

the first time you meet someone, your name appears on your genie uniform so that they know who you are

dry-clean only

Chameleon uniform

Lexie rolled her eyes. 'You do need to wash it occasionally, Jake.'

'What are those other tweenies waiting for?' asked Poppy.

'For their mentors,' said Lexie. 'You see, every Stage Two genie has a Three assigned to look after them. Your mentor shows you around and answers any questions you have. They will be like a big brother or sister to you. It's an old tradition at this school.' Lexie looked at her watch with a frown. 'Actually, where are the mentors? They should be here by now.'

'Look out!' yelled Jake suddenly. Poppy turned to see the air thick with magic carpets, all flying in formation.

'Ah, finally,' said Lexie. 'The mentors.' One carpet in particular seemed to be making

a beeline for them. It came so low that Poppy had to duck as it flew over her head. The carpet screeched to a halt mid-air, and then landed with a *whoomp* at Lexie's feet. A boy and a girl jumped off.

'Hi there,' said the boy, grinning and straightening his turban. 'I'm Santino.'

'Hello, Santino. I'm Princess Alexandria,' said Lexie, smiling.

Santino paled and immediately did an awkward-looking bow. 'Sorry we're late, Your Royal Genieness – we had carpet troubles,' he said. 'I'm Jake's mentor.'

Poppy liked the look of Santino straight away. His face was cheeky but it was also kind.

'And this is Poppy's mentor, Zara,' said Santino, gesturing to the girl. Zara had bright blue eyes and glossy blonde hair that fell in

~Zara~

curls from her high ponytail. When Poppy smiled at her, she didn't smile back. In fact, she gave Poppy a *very* unfriendly look.

Taken aback, Poppy turned to Santino. 'How do you know our names?' she asked, ignoring Zara for the moment.

'Because they're written on your uniforms,' he chuckled.

Looking down, Poppy saw that Santino was right. Her name had suddenly appeared

in purple letters on the front of her uniform. The same happened to Jake. 'I'm sure those weren't there before,' she said.

Lexie nodded. 'When you first start at Genie High, your name lights up if you meet someone new. Once you all know each other, it fades for good.'

'I would've recognised you anyway, Poppy,' said Santino. 'You're Golden, aren't you?'

'Yep, she sure is,' said Jake proudly.

'Jake!' said Poppy. The funny feeling in her tummy came back with a rush.

Jake shrugged his shoulders. 'What?' he said. 'I didn't tell him. He already knew.'

Santino grinned. 'Everyone knows who you are. You're totally famous. Lots of people are really excited to meet you.'

'Huh,' muttered Zara so softly that only

Poppy heard her. 'There's no way *I'm* going to get excited about some Golden goody-goody who thinks she knows it all.'

Poppy froze. No-one had ever called her a goody-goody before. It was so unfair, especially as Zara didn't even know her yet!

I'm going to show Zara that she's wrong about me, Poppy decided. *I am NOT a goody-goody*. She wasn't sure how she would do this exactly but she was determined to work it out.

'I've got to get going,' said Lexie, giving Poppy a goodbye hug. She tried to give one to Jake too, but he wiggled away.

'No hugs!' he said.

'OK, then,' laughed Lexie. 'I hope you both enjoy yourselves. But work hard, too.'

Poppy's heart sank a little as Lexie vanished in a puff of smoke. It was going to be weird

without her around. For a moment, Poppy felt like crying, but she forced the tears to stop. She was determined to have a fantastic first day at Genie High.

'So,' said Santino, while Zara inspected her nails. 'Any questions?'

'Only about five billion,' said Jake.

Santino chuckled. 'Come on, then. We're supposed to show you the Turquoise Bottle first. You can ask me questions there.'

Poppy hoped she could ask Santino questions too. Somehow she didn't think Zara was going to be very helpful.

The Turquoise Bottle reminded Poppy of the Stage One Training Centre. It was very comfortable and although Santino told them

it was a classroom, it looked nothing like a normie one. Instead of desks and chairs, there were large, comfortable cushions. Small magic carpets flew around, with snacks for whenever the students were peckish.

Over in the corner, there were two silver rubbish bins whispering and giggling to themselves. Poppy got the feeling they might be rather cheeky.

'This is where you'll do some of your compulsory classes,' Santino explained. 'You have to do them to graduate from Stage Two to Stage Three. Ancient Genie Languages, Advanced Wish Granting and Carpet Control are compulsory – but there are heaps of other classes you can *choose* to do as well.'

'Like what?' asked Jake.

Santino pushed a button on his Dial-Up and

showed them a list. Poppy leant over to see. 'Smoke Painting, Genie Judo, Hover-dance,' she read aloud, her eyes growing wider and wider. 'Wow. They all sound so fun! How do you even choose which ones to go to?'

'Your Dial-Up has been programmed with your personality profile,' said Santino, 'so when a class is coming up it thinks you'll like, it reminds you.'

'Hey, boothead, genie football tryouts are on tomorrow,' chimed in Jake's Dial-Up. 'You might even make the team if you manage to kick the ball straight for once!'

'Hey, that's *Jake* to you, button-face,' Jake growled at his Dial-Up. He looked at Santino. 'Is there such a thing as genie football?'

Santino nodded. 'We play it in the Football Oval Bottle.'

'Wow,' said Jake. 'There must be hundreds of different bottles here.'

'There are!' said Santino. 'There's a Theatre Bottle and a Gym Bottle. There's even a Velodrome Bottle where we do carpet riding. Plus there are a whole bunch of *secret* bottles that we –'

'That's enough, Santino!' snapped Zara. Poppy jumped. She'd forgotten Zara was there!

'Sorry, Zara,' Santino muttered sheepishly. Then his face brightened again. 'Come on. I'll take you to the Carpet Bottle.'

When he'd turned away, Jake nudged Poppy, his eyes twinkling. He didn't speak, but Poppy knew exactly what he was thinking, because she was thinking the same thing.

They had to learn more about those *secret* bottles!

The Carpet Bottle was stacked high with magic carpets of all shapes and sizes. Some of them were quite tiny and covered in delicate floral patterns. Others were very large with intricate swirling designs.

Santino lead them over to the plainest, heaviest-looking pile. He rifled through them and pulled out two. 'These are nice slow beginners' carpets,' he said, while Zara stood there looking bored. 'They've been sprayed with Go Slow to make them easy to control.'

'Poppy has her own carpet,' Jake piped up. '*And* she can ride already.'

Poppy flushed. She knew Jake was trying to be nice, but she really wished he'd stop boasting about her! It would only convince

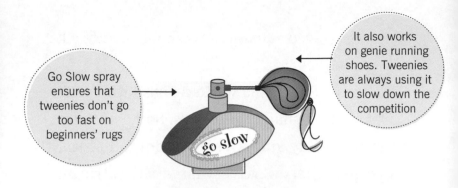

Go Slow spray ensures that tweenies don't go too fast on beginners' rugs

It also works on genie running shoes. Tweenies are always using it to slow down the competition

go slow

Zara that Poppy *was* some know-it-all goody-goody.

'I've still got heaps of stuff to learn,' she muttered, tucking the beginner's carpet under her arm. Rocket wriggled with annoyance in her backpack. Poppy could tell he hated the idea of her riding another carpet.

'So, you're a natural, huh?' sneered Zara. 'I can't wait to see you in action.'

'You won't be disappointed,' said Jake, not seeming to notice that Zara was being nasty.

Then he winked at Poppy. 'You might even pick up a few tips, Zara,' he added innocently.

Zara sneered and tossed her blonde ponytail.

'Actually, Zara is probably the best rider at Genie High,' explained Santino hastily. 'And she knows almost as much about magic carpets as our principal, Lady Topaz.'

Poppy's Dial-Up coughed politely. 'Speaking of Lady Topaz, it's time to go to the Velodrome Bottle for your first Carpet Control class. It's not a good idea to keep Lady Topaz waiting. I'll take you now, if you like. No hassle at all. In fact, it'd be my honour to escort such a wondrous genie as you.'

'Great, let's go,' said Poppy, putting her thumb on the send button.

Chapter 4

A moment later, Poppy found herself standing in a vast green bottle with a huge track in the middle. The track looked a bit like a running track and was surrounded with tiered seating. Other Stage Two tweenies and their mentors had started filling the stands.

'The Velodrome Bottle is where we learn to fly,' explained Santino. 'We also have school assemblies in here.'

Poppy looked up. The top of the bottle

seemed so far away. 'I'd love to fly right up there and then come zooming back down again,' she grinned.

'That's against school rules,' said Zara. 'And I'm sure you wouldn't want to break any of those, you know, being all boring and *Golden*.'

Poppy frowned. Like all genies, she had a quick temper and Zara kept saying things to fire it up. *But it wouldn't be good if I had a fight with my mentor*, thought Poppy. So she took a deep breath. 'Just because I'm a Golden genie doesn't mean I'm boring,' she replied, as calmly as she could.

'Yeah, knowing everything and being perfect sounds like *heaps* of fun,' said Zara, rolling her eyes.

Poppy felt her anger burbling up again.

What was *with* this girl? But before she could say anything, Jake bounded over, full of excitement. He pointed to a television screen hovering against the wall of the velodrome. 'Have you checked out the moves the genies are pulling on that video?' he said, shaking his head in disbelief.

Poppy looked up. The video showed genies zooming around at top speed, sliding up and down the walls and doing dangerous-looking turns. Then a blonde girl flashed across the screen, doing a triple mid-air loop without even slowing down.

'Wow! Was that you, Zara?' said Poppy, immediately forgetting how cross she'd felt a moment ago.

Zara shrugged. 'Yes,' she said. 'But that clip is old. I'm much better now.'

'The genies in the video are the top riders at our school,' said Santino. 'It's supposed to inspire everyone else.'

Poppy caught Jake's eye and grinned. She couldn't wait for her first proper riding class to start, even if she did have to use a boring beginner's carpet!

Then she slipped her hand into her backpack and gave Rocket a tickle. 'I'll take you for a ride really soon,' she told him. It had been ages since she'd gone riding. She'd flown Rocket around her bedroom once, but she ended up knocking all her books off her shelves so she didn't try it again. It was too risky.

Rocket tried to wriggle out of her bag in response.

'Did you learn to ride on *that* thing?' said

Zara suddenly, pointing at Rocket.

'Yes,' said Poppy. 'Why?'

'Well, no wonder you didn't fall off,' smirked Zara. 'That old thing probably goes at a snail's pace. You're not a natural. You've just had beginner's luck.'

'It wasn't *beginner's* luck,' Jake said indignantly. 'Poppy is an awesome rider. She rode for the first time without any lessons at all, *and* she's Golden, so she's can do heaps of advanced stuff. She probably won't even need to do the beginners' class, right, Poppy?'

'Shh, Jake!' muttered Poppy, through gritted teeth.

But Jake shook his head. 'I bet you're as good a rider as Zara,' he insisted. 'Maybe even better.'

The seats were almost full of Twos and Threes now, and they were all staring at Jake and Poppy.

Zara narrowed her eyes. 'Is that a challenge, Goldie?'

'Hang on,' protested Poppy. 'I never said anything! Listen, Zara, I just want to go to the beginners' class and –'

Jake butted in. 'If you guys had a race, I bet Poppy would win,' he declared. Poppy glared at him. Was he *trying* to make Zara hate her more?

Santino whistled. 'A Two racing a Three? And not just any Three, but *Zara*,' he said. 'That's brave.'

'Brave or totally *stupid*,' said Zara, shaking her head. 'But hey, Goldie, if you want to race, how about we –'

Before Zara could finish, there was a puff of bright orange smoke nearby and a grand-looking genie appeared before them. She was seated on a gnarled old wooden chair with lion's feet, which seemed to be *purring*.

The genie was dressed in what looked like leaves and flowers woven together in intricate patterns. It was the most beautiful dress Poppy had ever seen. The genie seemed old, although her face was very young and her dark brown hair didn't have a single streak of grey in it.

It's her eyes, thought Poppy. *She looks like she's seen heaps of incredible things.*

'That's Lady Topaz,' whispered Santino. 'She's been the principal here for about a thousand years and she likes to be obeyed. Better find a seat quickly.'

Poppy hurried to a chair. It wasn't that Lady Topaz looked mean, but she definitely looked like she was used to tweenies paying her their full attention.

Once everyone was sitting, Lady Topaz's chair bounded quickly on its wooden feet until it was positioned in front of the seated tweenies. Then it stood there, purring quietly while Lady Topaz spoke.

'Welcome, new tweenies, to Genie High,' said Lady Topaz, in a voice so rich she almost seemed to be singing rather than speaking.

'I'm sure you're all very excited about your first day at Genie High, and I hope your mentors have made you feel welcome.'

Poppy suppressed a snort. *Her* mentor had done exactly the opposite! *Maybe I could change mentors?* she thought, glancing around her. All the other Threes looked so nice!

'And now it's time to begin your very first class at Genie High,' Lady Topaz went on. 'I see that you've all been assigned your very first magic carpet, and I'm sure you're all keen to start flying – so in a moment I will ask your mentors to take you through some basics.' The room started buzzing with excitement. Everyone clearly liked this idea a lot!

'Excuse me, Lady Topaz,' said Zara suddenly. All the tweenies turned to stare, and Poppy looked at Zara nervously. What

56

was she going to say?

'What should we do if our Two is too advanced for the beginners' class?' said Zara loudly. 'Poppy says that she can already ride and she'd rather use her own carpet than our slow beginner ones.'

Instantly a murmur rippled through the crowd. 'That's Poppy Miller – the Golden genie!' whispered someone behind Poppy.

'I heard she was nice,' muttered someone else. 'But maybe she's a show-off.'

Poppy's face burned with embarrassment. She didn't want to be the centre of attention like this! She glared furiously at Zara, who smiled back smugly.

Lady Topaz frowned. 'All our carpets have been personally selected by me,' she said. 'They go at exactly the speed they are

57

supposed to go. And I'm sure there are some things you can learn from the beginners' class, Poppy, even if you are Golden.'

Poppy nodded. 'I know there are heaps of things I can learn,' she said loudly, hoping everyone heard her.

Then Lady Topaz's face softened. 'Why don't you and Zara come out the front first?' she suggested. 'You seem eager to learn how to fly. Zara, you can show Poppy some of the basics.'

Poppy grabbed her beginner's carpet and followed Zara down to the centre of the velodrome. She felt very nervous, knowing that everyone was watching her.

Barely disguising her boredom, Zara told Poppy to lay the carpet down and then showed her how to sit so she was properly balanced.

Poppy had worked out how to do these things already, but she pretended she didn't know.

'Now, tap the carpet lightly in front of you,' instructed Zara, 'and say *up*.'

Poppy did what Zara said and sure enough, the carpet rose up. All the tweenies clapped.

'Wonderful, Poppy,' said Lady Topaz. 'Now bring it down again and everyone else can have a try.'

But just then, a violent shiver rolled through the training rug and instead of sinking to the floor, it rose higher. Poppy only just managed to grab hold before the carpet took off with a *whoosh*.

'Down, carpet, DOWN!' commanded Lady Topaz.

But Poppy's carpet didn't take any notice. It whizzed wildly around the velodrome,

seemingly intent on shaking Poppy off. She held on tightly and, once she'd recovered from the surprise of the carpet's sudden departure, she felt a grin creep across her face.

'Don't bother trying to shake me off,' she whispered to the carpet. 'I'm not going anywhere. So let's just have some fun.'

Straight away, the carpet seemed to relax a little, but it didn't slow down. In fact, it went faster than ever. Poppy crouched down low and held on tight. It felt great to be riding again – and at top speed too! She caught a glimpse of the tweenies down below, cheering and clapping, and she grinned even wider.

'Poppy, don't panic,' called Lady Topaz. 'I'm coming up to get you.'

Poppy saw the worried look on the principal's face. She sighed. It was time for

the fun to end. 'Down,' she commanded the rug, and the carpet slipped down until came to rest right in front of Lady Topaz.

Lady Topaz grabbed Poppy's arm, like she was worried the carpet would take off again. 'I'm so sorry, Poppy,' she said, looking puzzled. 'That's never happened before. This carpet mustn't have been sprayed properly with Go Slow.'

'I'm fine, Lady Topaz,' said Poppy, smiling. 'I actually enjoyed it.'

Lady Topaz nodded thoughtfully. 'You did very well,' she said. 'It's clear that you do have some natural riding talent. Can you show me your own carpet?'

Poppy tugged Rocket out of her backpack. Lady Topaz looked at Rocket in surprise. 'This is a very ancient rug,' she said softly.

'Very ancient indeed. Where did you get it?'

'Lexie – er, I mean, Princess Alexandria gave it to me,' said Poppy.

Lady Topaz nodded. 'Ah. Of course she did. That makes sense. And now I can see why you want to ride it. I'm going to allow it. From tomorrow you can join the intermediate Carpet Control class instead of the beginners', but I expect you to pay attention.'

'Thanks, Lady Topaz,' said Poppy, delighted. Rocket would be so pleased!

But her pleasure soon faded. As she and Zara walked back to their seats, Poppy heard one of the tweenies whisper, 'You were right. Golden genies *are* show-offs.'

'Well, maybe,' another tweenie whispered back. 'But to be fair, that carpet did go pretty crazy on her.'

Poppy felt a thump of discomfort – but after the rush of her carpet ride, she was also feeling determined. Even though Zara was a pain, Poppy wouldn't let her ruin Genie High. One way or another she'd show everyone that Poppy Miller was no different to any other student at this school.

Chapter 5

'So, what do you think of Poppy's riding now?' Jake asked Zara smugly when the Carpet Control class had finished.

Zara shrugged. 'I still say she's just a very lucky beginner,' she said, glancing at her Dial-Up. 'Time to go, Santino. Oh, and Goldie,' she said, turning to Poppy, 'if you really want to prove you can ride, how about you compete in the next Bottle Hop?'

'Definitely!' said Jake quickly.

'Excellent,' said Zara. Then she pressed a button on her Dial-Up. With a burst of green sparks, she and Santino disappeared.

Poppy glared at Jake. 'What have you gotten me in to?' she groaned. 'We don't even know what a Bottle Hop is.'

'So what?' said Jake, his eyes twinkling. 'It sounds like fun! I can't wait for Zara to see how good a rider you are.'

Then their Dial-Ups started beeping. 'Oh, Most Honourable and Wondrous Tweenie,' Poppy's Dial-Up chanted. 'Your Wish Granting class is starting in the Turquoise Bottle.'

'Yeah, so get your lazy bones down there,' added Jake's Dial-Up with a cheeky giggle.

Jake shook his head. 'I have to change that voice setting,' he muttered. 'And soon.'

65

Lots of other tweenies were already in the Turquoise Bottle when Poppy and Jake arrived. They were staring at Poppy and whispering.

Even though she felt a little shy, and more than a little embarrassed, Poppy decided to go up to them. *The sooner they get to know me,* she told herself, pulling Jake along with her. *the sooner they'll realise I'm no goody-goody.*

When she got there, she took a deep breath and smiled at them. 'Hi, I'm Poppy, and this is Jake,' she said. 'And I guess you're all staring at me either because I have something gross hanging from my nose, or because I'm a Golden genie. But I'm really no different to anyone else here. I'm just a normal tweenie.'

One of the girls smiled back shyly. 'Um, Poppy,' she said, as the name Alyssa flashed

up on her uniform, 'I have a question. Why are you even at this school? I mean, you obviously already know how to fly, and I've heard that you can even grant wishes.'

'I was wondering that, too,' said a boy called Nathan. 'Are you just here to keep an eye on us or something? If you already know everything, what's the point of being here?'

Poppy shook her head firmly. 'No!' she

said. 'I am definitely *not* here to spy on you guys. And I *don't* know everything. That flying thing today – I just held on.'

'But you've granted wishes, haven't you?' persisted Alyssa.

'Well, yes,' Poppy admitted. 'But I had no idea what I was doing. It was pretty embarrassing, actually – my sister found my genie bottle.'

'Oh no!' groaned Alyssa. 'That's terrible!'

'I know,' Poppy said, rolling her eyes. Then she explained the whole story about how Astrid had wished to be famous. By the time Poppy had finished, everyone was laughing.

'I'm glad you told us about that,' said Nathan, grinning at her. 'I thought you were going to be a total goody-goody, you know. But I guess you make mistakes too.'

68

Poppy laughed. 'Believe me. I make *heaps* of mistakes,' she said. 'It took me ages to even learn how to levitate!'

Suddenly there was a puff of silver smoke, and a genie with shimmering white hair appeared before them. 'Hello Twos, I'm Madame Pearl,' she said with a warm smile. 'Sit down please, and let's start our Wish Granting class.'

Poppy and the others grabbed some cushions and sat down.

'Now,' said Madame Pearl. 'Let's find out what you already know. Let's see ... Poppy, can you tell me how to grant a wish?'

'You do your wish routine,' said Poppy, 'and imagine the wish coming true.'

'And what is a wish routine, exactly?' asked Madame Pearl.

69

'Well, it's kind of like a dance,' said Poppy, remembering what she'd learnt in her Stage One training. 'Every genie has their own personal routine. You have to find out what this routine is by yourself. Sometimes the moves can be pretty unusual.'

Jake grinned at Poppy when she said this, and Poppy knew why. Her own wish routine had a very strange movement in it – she touched her nose with her tongue. It was a trick she'd been doing ever since she was very young. Poppy had never realised that one day it would help her to grant wishes!

'And can you tell me whether a genie should grant any human wish straight away?' said Madame Pearl.

'We're supposed to find a way of *not* granting the wish,' recited Poppy, 'because

70

normies make such bad wishes. We can also use Wish Twisting. That's when we spin the normie's wish around so that it ends up being something they don't really want at all.'

'Very good, Poppy,' said Madame Pearl approvingly.

Poppy felt pleased until she noticed a tweenie called Lisa rolling her eyes. Poppy bit her lip. *Oops!* she thought, sinking into her cushion a little further. *No wonder they think I'm a goody-goody.*

Madame Pearl cleared her throat. 'Now in this class we are going to look at advanced wish-granting techniques,' she went on. 'Make sure you pay attention and absorb everything I say. You never know when this information might come in handy.' Madame Pearl swirled her finger through the air. A trail of purplish

smoke appeared where her finger had been, forming words. The words 'Wish Leading' hung in mid-air for a moment, then gradually faded away.

Everyone opened their genie jotters and started taking notes.

'Wish Leading is a more complex form of Wish Twisting,' Madame Pearl explained. 'We use it when we want a normie to waste their wishes on something that's easy to grant.'

A few of the tweenies looked confused. Madame Pearl smiled. 'Have you noticed how often normies say the words "I wish"?' she said. 'They might say, "I wish I had a sandwich," or, "I wish I could find my keys". You can probably see that these wishes are very easy to grant. You could grant them without the normie even knowing you were a

genie! That's what Wish Leading is all about.'

Then Madame Pearl looked around. 'Does anyone have any ideas on how you could "lead" a wish?'

Everyone was silent. Poppy thought of some things straight away, but this time she was determined to keep quiet. She didn't want to look like a know-it-all again.

After a moment or two, Madame Pearl smiled at her. 'What about you, Poppy?'

Poppy could feel everyone watching her, waiting to see if she would give the correct answer. 'Well,' she said, thinking quickly, 'you could beckon with your finger and say, "Here, wishy-wishy-wish! I want to lead you!".' The class tittered, and Poppy felt a rush of satisfaction.

Madame Pearl shook her head. 'Not quite.

Anyone else?'

Nathan put up his hand. 'You could ask heaps of really annoying questions until the normie said, "I wish you'd stop that".'

'Or you could keep accidentally-on-purpose bumping into them until they said, "I wish you'd go away",' said Alyssa.

Madame Pearl nodded. 'Those are both excellent suggestions.'

I knew that stuff anyway, Poppy thought, feeling pleased. *But let's see who calls me a know-it-all now*!

'The other thing we will talk about is Coincidences,' continued Madame Pearl, writing the word in the air. 'Coincidences are another useful way of disguising a wish when the normie you're granting it for doesn't know you're a genie.'

'How is that possible?' asked Jake, looking surprised. 'Isn't it pretty obvious that you're a genie if you've popped out of a bottle in front of them?'

Madame Pearl raised an eyebrow. 'Tell me, did any of you believe it when *you* first saw a genie?'

'Well, no,' admitted Poppy. 'I thought it was a big joke.'

Madame Pearl nodded. 'Exactly,' she said. 'You'd be surprised how often people refuse to believe what is happening right in front of their eyes. Especially adult normies. But a clever genie will use this to their advantage. If a normie doesn't believe you're a genie, they probably won't demand wishes. And if they do accidentally make a wish, it's much easier for you to disguise it as a coincidence.'

Then Madame Pearl wrote 'Secret Wishes' in the air. 'This is the final thing we'll talk about today,' she said. 'Granting wishes secretly – so that the normie has no idea you're doing it – is an invaluable genie skill. Perhaps you want to disguise a wish as a coincidence. This is all very well, but what will the normie think if you suddenly start flinging yourself about, doing your wish routine? It might make them a little suspicious, correct?'

Everyone nodded and Madame Pearl lowered her voice. 'That's why we have another, much less conspicuous way of granting wishes.'

Poppy and the other tweenies leant forward on their cushions, waiting to hear what she was going to say.

'You close your eyes and you concentrate

very carefully on imagining the wish coming true,' said Madame Pearl softly, 'and then you say the special, genie magic word.' She looked around the room mysteriously. 'Can anyone guess what that magic word is?'

Poppy's mind had gone blank, and it looked as though everyone else's had too. Then Madame Pearl wrote a word up in the air with smoke letters. It shimmered there while everyone stared at it in astonishment.

Please

'Please?' blurted Jake in disbelief. 'The genie magic word is *please?*'

Madame Pearl laughed. 'That's right. You've probably been asked thousands of times by adult normies what the "magic word" is – and none of them know just how magic that word is if it's uttered by a genie.'

Looking around, Poppy could see that the other tweenies were as surprised as she was! Everyone started talking excitedly among themselves, until finally, Madame Pearl raised her hand. 'That's enough for today, everyone. I'll see you in the Sapphire Bottle for your Ancient Genie Languages lesson tomorrow morning. But before I go, let's do one more important piece of revision. What is the most important thing a genie can do to avoid having to grant wishes?'

The tweenies chanted the answer in unison. 'Keep your genie bottle well hidden!'

Madame Pearl nodded. 'Correct,' she said as they packed up their books. 'If the normies can't find your bottle, they can't ask for wishes – and that saves everyone a lot of bother.'

Luckily my bottle is well hidden under the bed,

thought Poppy as she put her jotter into her backpack.

Then Poppy frowned. She *had* remembered to put the bottle back under her bed, hadn't she? As soon as she thought this, a queasy feeling rose in her stomach – the one that she'd felt when Astrid had found her genie bottle and started demanding wishes. And when Poppy's fingers started feeling tingly, she knew for sure what was going on.

Oh no, she thought, filled with dread. Someone had discovered her bottle, and she was being drawn back into the normie world – but by who?

Chapter 6

'I really hope Astrid hasn't found my bottle again,' muttered Poppy as she whooshed back to the normie world. Her sister had treated her like a slave!

'Don't worry,' murmured her Dial-Up, sounding a little rattled by the journey. 'Genies can only grant three wishes to any one normie.'

When Poppy arrived back in her bedroom in a puff of smoke, she saw her mother lying

on the ground with her head under the bed, pulling things out and muttering crossly. The middle of the room was piled high with Poppy's old shoes, scrunched up school assignments and clothes she no longer wore.

Then Poppy spotted something else – not on the floor, but sitting on her bedside table. Her genie bottle! *Mum must have found it*, realised Poppy, her stomach sinking.

She checked her uniform. It had changed back to a normie one, just like Lexie said it would. She stepped closer to her mum. 'Hi, Mum,' said Poppy, trying to sound as normal as she could.

'Poppy! What are you doing here?' asked her mum, pulling her head out from under the bed.

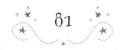

'I'm home from school,' Poppy replied. 'You know – the school I got a full scholarship to because I'm so smart?'

Poppy hoped that reminding her mum of this would put her in a good mood. It didn't.

'Well, I hope they'll teach you how to tidy up after yourself,' her mum said, sounding annoyed. 'Your room is a disgrace. Look at all the things I found under your bed.' She picked up Poppy's genie bottle. 'Why is this under there? It's such a pretty bottle, but it's covered with dust that just won't come off!'

Poppy's mind whirled into action. *Mum could make a wish at any time*, she thought. *I have to be ready!*

Then she remembered the class she had just taken. *Maybe I can use that wish-leading technique Madame Pearl was talking about.*

Poppy wasn't really sure how it worked, but it couldn't hurt to try.

'Is there something you *wish* I would do, Mum?' asked Poppy innocently. 'To help with the tidying up, I mean.'

'Well,' sighed her mum, 'I do really wish you'd start putting your dirty clothes in the washing basket.'

Poppy grinned. It had worked perfectly! Poppy picked up a dirty T-shirt and one sock and dumped them in the washing basket.

'What do you wish I would do now, Mum?' said Poppy

Her mum frowned. 'There are still lots of clothes on the floor, Poppy.'

'But you only wished I would *start* picking them up,' Poppy pointed out. 'Do you wish I would *finish* picking them up now?'

'I'm not in the mood for jokes, Poppy,' her mum snapped. 'You're a tweenager now, not a child.'

Suddenly Poppy felt crabby too. 'You always treat me like a child,' she complained, 'so I may as well act like one! Astrid is allowed to do heaps more things than I am.'

'Well that's because Astrid is ...' Poppy's mum's voice trailed off.

'Older,' Poppy said grumpily. 'It's not fair. Astrid will *always* be older and I'll never catch up. She's allowed to do all kinds of things I'm not allowed to do. And you give her everything she asks for. When Astrid asked for a guinea pig, she got one. But when I asked for a bird-eating spider, you said no!'

To be fair, Poppy had only asked for a bird-

eating spider because she knew she wouldn't be allowed to have one.

'Oh Poppy,' her mother said. She sighed. 'I wish I could be the perfect mother, Poppy. I really do.'

Poppy stood still, staring at her mum. 'You *wish* you could be the perfect mother?'

'Yes,' said her mum. 'But to be honest, Poppy, I don't know what that is.'

A smile crept across Poppy's face. *Actually,* she thought, *I might have an idea!* Remembering what Madame Pearl had said about granting wishes secretly, Poppy closed her eyes and concentrated on her mum becoming *perfect.* Then she said the magic word ...

'What are you saying "please" for?' asked her mum. But even as she spoke, a confused expression came over her mum's face, like she

85

wasn't sure where she was. Or *who* she was.

Two seconds later, her expression had totally changed again. Poppy's mum smiled brightly. 'You know,' she said with a wink, 'I think we should go and get you that bird-eating spider after all. After a celebratory ice-cream, of course.'

'Right now?' said Poppy, astonished.

'Yes,' said her mum, grabbing her car keys. 'Don't worry about homework. A super-student like you deserves to take it easy once in a while.' And then she whisked Poppy out of the house.

Poppy's mum stopped the car on the main road, in front of the new ice-cream shop. Poppy had been dying to go there but her

mum had always refused.

That afternoon, however, she linked her arm through Poppy's and led her through the door. 'What would you like?' she asked Poppy. 'Pick anything from the menu. We're celebrating!'

'Really?' said Poppy. Normally her mum wouldn't let her eat ice-cream this close to dinner time.

'Of course!' beamed her mum. 'Get something large and covered in chocolate syrup.'

Poppy shrugged. 'OK,' she said, and chose one called a Chocolate Avalanche. It was something that her old mum would have never let her have.

The first few mouthfuls tasted amazing. But halfway through it, Poppy started to feel sick. She pushed the ice-cream away.

87

'I can't finish it,' she admitted.

Usually Poppy's mum would've been cross with Poppy for ordering something too big. But today, she just shrugged. 'No problem, honey-bun,' she said affectionately. 'Let's buy a tub for tonight, shall we?'

'I don't think I'll have room,' said Poppy, her tummy gurgling. Just the thought of

eating more ice-cream was making her feel queasy.

'There's *always* room for ice-cream!' laughed her mum, selecting an extra-large tub of triple chocolate chip. 'You can finish it off for breakfast if you don't get through it all tonight. Come on. Let's go to the pet shop now and get that bird-eating spider you've always wanted.'

'Maybe we should forget about that, Mum,' said Poppy, hurrying along beside her mother. She wasn't sure that she wanted a bird-eating spider after all.

'Forget it?' exclaimed her mum. 'Certainly not. I won't rest until you have that spider snuggled safe in your arms. It will make a wonderful pet. I've heard they grow as large as dinner plates!'

Poppy shuddered. 'Where would I keep it?'

'Just let it run around in your bedroom,' her mum chuckled. 'It can sleep on your pillow.'

'Oh,' said Poppy, biting her lip. 'Right.' She'd actually suggested this herself once. But she didn't think her mum would ever agree to it. She did *not* want a huge spider sleeping on her pillow!

The pet shop was closed when Poppy and her mum arrived. 'Come on,' said Poppy, relieved. 'Let's go home.'

But Poppy's mum started banging on the door until a man appeared. 'Sorry, we're shut,' he said politely.

'I want to buy a bird-eating spider,' said Poppy's mum loudly, completely ignoring him. Poppy wanted to sink through the

90

ground with embarrassment. Her mum was never normally this rude.

'Well, I *do* have one of those available at the moment,' said the man slowly. 'Come back tomorrow morning and you can buy it.'

He started to close the door, but Poppy's mum put her foot in it. 'Not tomorrow,' she said petulantly. 'Now.'

Poppy tugged her mum's arm. 'Come on, Mum,' she said. 'I can wait.'

But her mum folded her arms. 'I'm not leaving until this man sells us that spider,' she said, sticking out her bottom lip in a pout.

Finally the man rolled his eyes. 'OK, fine,' he said. 'Wait one moment.'

He went back into the shop and came back a few minutes later with a clear plastic box that had holes in the side. There was a large

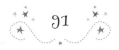

ball of shredded paper in the middle, which the spider was hiding beneath. The pet shop man handed the box to Poppy. 'Her name is Bertha,' he said. 'She needs fresh meat twice a day and make sure you tickle her tummy bristles occasionally. She loves that.'

Poppy's mouth went dry. The last thing she wanted to do was tickle a spider! In fact, she didn't want to do anything with the spider except give it straight back to the pet shop.

But before she knew what was happening, her mum had paid the man and Poppy found herself the not-so-proud owner of Bertha the bird-eating spider.

On the way home, Mrs Miller insisted on stopping at a DVD shop and choosing a big

pile of DVDs for Poppy. They were all ones that Poppy had pestered her mum to let her watch in the past, but which she was always told were too scary or too grown-up. Poppy walked around carrying Bertha's box very carefully. She didn't want to do anything that would cause the spider to come scuttling out.

By the time they got home, Poppy was exhausted – but her mum was full of energy. She bounded off to the living room with the stack of DVDs. 'Let's stay up late watching these and eating ice-cream,' her mum yelled over her shoulder. 'How about some popcorn for dinner?'

Usually Poppy would have loved to watch a DVD with her mum. But this strange lady wasn't her mum. This person was behaving more like an annoying little kid!

'I'm too tired tonight,' Poppy said, yawning. 'I've got school tomorrow, remember?'

'Oh, don't worry about silly old *school*,' said her mum, who was now jumping up and down on the sofa. 'I've been thinking – how about we change things around so that you go to school two days a week and have a five-day weekend?'

Poppy shook her head. 'I like my new school, Mum,' she said. 'I'm going to bed. Maybe we can watch a DVD tomorrow.'

Finally, after twenty minutes of her mum trying to make her play board games, Poppy managed to escape to her room. But even though she was worn out, Poppy couldn't sleep. She had placed Bertha's box on the far corner of her desk, and she could hear the spider moving around.

Maybe she's trying to escape, thought Poppy nervously. She could imagine the bird-eating spider crawling out of the box and creeping up onto her bed, and ...

After an hour of tossing and turning, Poppy sat up. *This is silly*, she thought, throwing the covers off. *I'm going to go sleep in my bottle.*

Her house had been fitted with an Excuse Generator so it wouldn't matter if she wasn't there in the morning. Excuse Generators were designed to make up excuses for those times when genies were in the genie realm and normies were looking for them. So Poppy put her toe at the entrance of the bottle and thought watery (if sleepy) thoughts.

Chapter 7

Poppy's genie bottle was such a comfortable, calm place to be. As soon as she arrived, Poppy looked at the mood dial on the wall and selected 'tropical beach at night'. Instantly, the lights dimmed and tiny, twinkling stars appeared. Palm trees seemed to grow from nowhere, and they were so realistic that Poppy was sure she could hear their leaves rustling. A gentle breeze blew around the bottle, scented with exotic flowers.

Yawning, Poppy climbed into her bed, which now looked like a hammock. *Next time I might try 'space float'*, she thought, as she drifted off to sleep. *Or maybe 'mermaid world'*...

Poppy woke up to the sound of someone humming one of her favourite songs. It was her Dial-Up.

The digital face gazed adoringly at her. 'Sorry to wake you, Oh Sleeping Tweenie of Extreme Marvellousness,' it said, 'but there's a Genie Judo class on in fifteen minutes. I thought you might like to go. Your Ancient Genie Languages class isn't until ten so you've got heaps of time.'

Poppy liked the idea of genie judo, but she was hungry too. 'It's a breakfast session,'

added the Dial-Up, seeming to know what she was thinking. 'There will be plenty to eat.'

Poppy sat up in her hammock and stretched. 'Sounds good,' she said, pressing send on her Dial-Up. Then she suddenly remembered how she had left her mum the night before. *I wonder if Excuse Generators can reverse wishes*, she thought hopefully.

When Poppy arrived in the Judo Bottle, she looked at her clothes. Sure enough, they had transformed into a white judo jacket, pants and a white belt. The bottle was already full of other Twos, including Nathan and Alyssa from her Wish Granting class. Alyssa was munching on a delicious-looking pastry.

'Where did you get that?' asked Poppy,

her tummy growling.

'From the buffet carpet,' explained Alyssa, pointing. Poppy looked over to see a large carpet, flying slowly around the outside of the room, laden with food. There were pastries, juices, fruit salad and even pancakes.

Poppy was just getting herself a blueberry pancake when Jake appeared. 'Hi, Jake,' she said. 'Did your Dial-Up suggest this class too?'

'I didn't *suggest* it,' snapped a nearby voice. 'I *ordered* him to go.'

Poppy raised an eyebrow, and Jake pulled a face. 'I changed my Dial-Up's voice profile to "bossy" by accident,' he said. 'And now it won't let me change it back.'

'That's right,' barked the Dial-Up. 'Bossy suits me just fine.'

Poppy snorted with laughter. 'Well, at least

it's not being cheeky anymore,' she pointed out, and took a big bite of her pancake.

The Genie Judo instructor was called Sensei Kicks. 'Genie judo is similar to normie judo,' he explained. 'But there's one important difference. It takes place in mid-air.'

Jake put up his hand. 'Will we get to throw each other over our shoulders?' he asked eagerly.

Sensei Kicks shook his head with a smile. 'You're not quite ready for that yet,' he said. 'Today we'll just do some exercises. We'll start on throwing in a few weeks.'

'Boring,' Jake muttered.

Sensei Kicks told everyone to sit down cross-legged on the ground. Then they levitated until

they were a metre off the ground. 'Now let's do our stretches up here,' said Sensei Kicks.

But when Sensei turned around, Jake nudged Poppy. 'Come on,' he whispered. 'Try and throw me over your shoulder! I bet you can't.'

Poppy hesitated. It would be fun to try, but Sensei Kicks had said they weren't ready yet. 'I'd better not,' she said.

'Why?' teased Jake. 'Because you're *Golden*?'

Out of the corner of her eye, Poppy saw Nathan and Alyssa, watching and listening. Poppy frowned. 'Yeah, right!' she said. Then, before she really knew what she was doing, Poppy grabbed Jake's arm – and a moment later he was sailing through the air above her head.

major
exercise

white belt
for
beginners

excellent
uniform

good
way to
practise
levitating

Genie judo

Jake was just as surprised as Poppy was when he found himself flat on his back ... but still floating in mid-air!

'Hey!' said Sensei Kicks, coming over. 'What do you think you're doing, Poppy?'

'Sorry,' said Poppy innocently. 'I was ... I was just shaking Jake's hand and I got a bit carried away.'

Alyssa and Nathan snickered. Sensei Kicks raised an eyebrow. 'That's some handshake you've got, Poppy,' he said.

Poppy grinned. 'You should see what happens when I wave!' she said.

'Show us!' giggled Alyssa.

But Sensei Kicks shook his head. 'No waving and no more hand-shaking either, thanks,' he said. His voice was stern, but there was a small smile at the corner of his mouth.

103

The sudden blast of an alarm made everyone jump. It was Jake's Dial-Up. 'Football tryouts start in five minutes,' it barked. 'Get a move on!'

Jake groaned. Sensei laughed. 'You'd better go,' he said. 'You wouldn't want to upset your Dial-Up.'

'That's right,' growled Jake's Dial-Up. 'You wouldn't.'

When the Genie Judo class finished, there was still an hour to go before Ancient Genie Languages. Poppy consulted her Dial-Up. 'You could go to Levi-dance,' it suggested, 'or try Astro-blading. You would be magnificent at both of them, Oh Most Excellent Tweenie with the Strong Muscles and Perfect Balance.'

'What's astro-blading?' asked Poppy, ignoring the compliment.

'It's like rollerblading, but you do it upside down,' her Dial-Up said eagerly. 'And levi-dancing is levitating and –'

'Or you could come to the Bottle Hop meeting,' said a voice behind her. It was Zara.

She looked at Poppy with one eyebrow raised. 'But maybe you're afraid of getting into trouble, Goldie?'

Poppy frowned. 'I'm not afraid!' she said crossly. 'Where's the Bottle Hop meeting?'

Zara smirked. 'It's in the Quartz Bottle. See you there.' Then she disappeared.

Straight away, Poppy scrolled through her Dial-Up's menu to find the Quartz Bottle.

'Excuse me,' said the Dial-Up nervously. 'I don't mean to doubt you, Oh Wise One, but is this really a good idea? Bottle Hopping is strictly forbidden at Genie High. And as a Golden genie, you're supposed to set a good example.'

Poppy sighed. The Dial-Up was starting to annoy her. 'It's just a meeting,' she said, pressing send. 'Don't worry.'

'If you say so,' said the Dial-Up doubtfully.

A few seconds later, Poppy found herself in a dimly lit bottle with a huge, dusty old chandelier hanging from the roof. The floor was so smooth that the glass glistened like a gemstone. Flying around the bottle were some Threes. They were going very fast and pulling off complicated-looking stunts with ease. Poppy spotted Santino among them, doing tricky loops.

Wow, thought Poppy. *These guys are amazing.*

Zara glided up beside her on a super-sleek carpet. 'You came, Goldie,' she said, with mock surprise. 'I thought you'd chicken out.'

Poppy tilted her chin up. 'I never chicken out,' she said firmly.

'Good,' said Zara, her eyes gleaming.

Another Bottle Hopper with red hair flew over and looked at Poppy suspiciously. 'Isn't she that Golden kid?' he said. 'Why did you bring her, Zara? She'll probably blab to Lady Topaz about this.'

'No, she won't, Louis,' said Santino, flying down to join them. 'Being Golden doesn't make her a dobber.'

Poppy glanced at Santino gratefully. It was nice that someone was sticking up for her.

'Does she even know *how* to ride?' asked someone else.

Right, thought Poppy, her annoyance taking over. *That's it!* Without saying a word, she pulled Rocket from her bag and jumped on. Rocket's tassels twitched with excitement, and Poppy only had to tap him lightly to make

him zoom off at top speed around the room, expertly dodging the other genies.

'Go, Poppy!' cheered Santino.

As she flew, Poppy felt her anger evaporate. Flying made her feel so good, especially when she was riding Rocket. 'Faster,' she urged, and her carpet obliged.

Poppy glanced around the room. She needed to do some kind of trick or stunt – something that would totally impress all these genies, and especially Zara. But what?

'Poppy!' shouted Santino. 'Look out!'

Poppy whipped her head around – just in time to see that she was headed straight for huge chandelier in the middle of the bottle. There was no time to swerve around it. All she could do was jump off Rocket and hope for the best!

Carpet riding

For a moment, Poppy was falling through the air. Then, as she fell past the chandelier, she managed to grab hold of a dangling tear-shaped crystal with one hand.

Rocket kept zooming forward as Poppy clung there, swinging from side to side. *I wonder how strong this thing is?* she thought nervously.

Even as she thought it, the crystal she was clinging to came loose and Poppy found herself plummeting once more. But not for long! She felt Rocket slide underneath her, breaking her fall.

Instantly all the Bottle Hoppers began cheering. Feeling a little shaky, Poppy brought Rocket down to the ground and gave him a pat. 'Thanks for saving me,' she whispered, as the Bottle Hoppers surrounded Poppy,

chattering with delight and amazement.

Louis shook her hand. 'Great flying,' he said with a grin. 'That stunt you did with the chandelier was awesome. I really thought you were going down.'

'Um, thanks,' said Poppy. She wasn't going to admit that it had been a mistake!

'You should definitely do the next Bottle Hop,' said Santino, clapping her on the back. 'You'll give Zara a good run!'

'That sounds great,' said Poppy, 'except that I have no idea what a Bottle Hop is.'

Then Zara stepped through the crowd of Bottle Hoppers, and everyone went quiet. All eyes turned to Zara, and she nodded. 'Welcome to the club, Goldie,' she said. 'You're ready to know now.'

Chapter 8

'Remember how Santino told you that there were secret bottles at this school?' said Zara, shooting Santino a withering look.

Poppy nodded. Of course she remembered!

'Well,' said Zara, 'Genie High is made up of hundreds of separate genie bottles. Some of them get used all the time – like the Turquoise Bottle and the Entrance Hall. But there are other destinations on the *official* bottle list that are hardly ever used.'

'Like this Quartz Bottle?' asked Poppy.

'Exactly,' said Zara. 'Which is why we Bottle Hoppers meet here.' Then she lowered her voice. 'But there are other bottles too. The most interesting ones aren't on the list at all.'

'Why aren't they on the list?' asked Poppy,

her eyes opened wide. She could feel the excitement bubbling up inside her, and it occurred to her that Zara wasn't being quite so awful as usual.

'They're ancient bottles that've been totally forgotten,' said Zara. 'Some of them haven't

been visited for hundreds of genie years, maybe even thousands. Bottle Hopping is a game that explores all those ancient places.'

'So how do we find them,' asked Poppy, 'if they're not even on the Dial-Up list?'

Zara leant forward and placed something heavy and cold in Poppy's hand. Poppy examined the object. 'It looks like a lid from a Location Lamp,' she said, 'except it has weird symbols instead of proper locations.'

Zara nodded. 'It's the lid from an ancient Location Lamp – one that the old tweenies at this school used to use to move from place to place. All those symbols indicate the ancient bottles. The lids are really rare, but we have managed to find two of them. They're the only way to get into – or out of – the ancient bottles. Here, pass me your Location Lamp.'

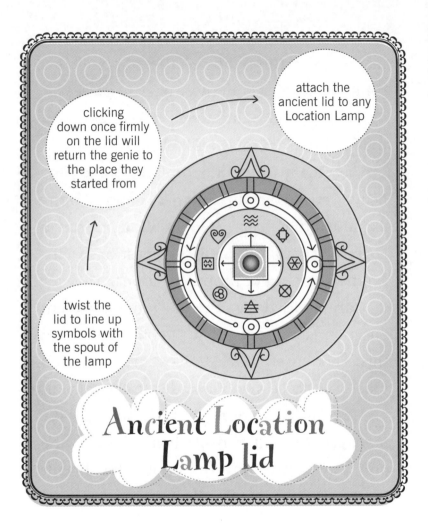

attach the ancient lid to any Location Lamp

clicking down once firmly on the lid will return the genie to the place they started from

twist the lid to line up symbols with the spout of the lamp

Ancient Location Lamp lid

Poppy took her lamp from her backpack and handed it over. Zara removed the lamp's lid and clipped on the ancient lid instead. Then she looked at Poppy coolly. 'Now it's ready for Bottle Hopping,' she said. 'If you're ready, of course. We could do it this afternoon.'

Poppy nodded, her eyes sparkling. 'I'm ready,' she said. 'Tell me how the game works.'

'You get twenty minutes to visit as many of the ancient bottles as you can,' explained Zara. 'We always take our carpets because then you can fly across the bottles and you see more. You need to take a quick video with your Dial-Up Device to prove you've been there. Then you hop to the next ancient bottle.' Zara shrugged. 'Easy.'

117

'Um, excuse me,' piped up a small voice. It was Poppy's Dial-Up. 'Sorry to be a party-pooper, but I must strongly advise you against this. Ancient bottles can be very dangerous. Some have powerful charms protecting them. And if you get lost in one, no-one will know where you are. You'll be lost in it forever.'

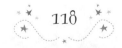

Zara groaned. 'Don't listen to that bunch of buttons, Poppy,' she said. 'I've done heaps of Bottle Hops and I've never seen anything dangerous. It's *fun*. The best bit is that you can fly as fast as you like because there's no-one to tell you to slow down. And if you do freak out about something then you can just click on the lamp's lid and it will take you straight back here. No problem.'

'It sounds pretty cool,' admitted Poppy. Secretly, she was feeling pleased that Zara wanted her to compete. *Maybe she's not so horrible after all*, Poppy thought.

'Don't do it, Poppy!' said the Dial-Up, sounding panicked. 'If Lady Topaz finds out about this you'll be expelled.'

Poppy hesitated. On the one hand, she wasn't sure it was worth risking expulsion just

to prove she wasn't perfect. She'd been dying to come to Genie High, and she really loved learning how to be a genie. But she was also sick of everyone thinking she was a goody-goody. Competing in a banned game seemed like the perfect way to change how people saw her.

Zara rolled her eyes. 'You can mute that thing, you know,' she said. 'Just press the red button. Unless you actually *want* to listen to it and be known as a totally boring goldie.'

Poppy frowned. 'I'm in,' she said loudly, and muted her Dial-Up. She wondered if she had accidentally changed the profile too. Her Dial-Up's digital face changed from polite to extremely grumpy, but it remained silent.

'You'll love the Bottle Hop,' said Santino, rubbing his hands together. 'It's awesome fun.'

Poppy's Dial-Up flashed. A message appeared on the screen.

Ancient Genie Languages starts in two minutes.

Not that you care about anything I have to say.

Regards, your Dial-Up.

Jake was already in the Sapphire Bottle when Poppy arrived. 'Hey!' said Poppy, grabbing a cushion next to him. 'How did the football tryouts go?'

'I made the team!' beamed Jake. 'So what have you been doing? Did you go to another class after Genie Judo?'

'That's great about the football team,' said

Poppy, trying to avoid the question. The Bottle Hop meeting was supposed to be a secret.

Jake looked at her through narrowed eyes. 'You're up to something,' he said. 'And if you don't tell me what, I'll start boasting about you being Golden again.'

'OK, OK,' said Poppy hastily. 'But you have to promise not to tell anyone.'

Jake grinned. 'Of course not! Now spill.'

But before Poppy could say a word, Madame Pearl arrived. 'I'll tell you later,' Poppy whispered as everyone quietened down.

Once she had everyone's attention, Madame Pearl began writing strange smoky squiggles in the air. 'This word is written in the ancient genie language of Swirl,' she said while she spun her fingers through the air. 'Genies don't really use it anymore, but Lady

122

Topaz feels that it's important for tweenies to learn – sort of like normies studying Latin. Now, can anyone tell me what this says?'

Poppy squinted at the smoky loops. It looked like a vapour trail made by a small out-of-control plane. But then, as she watched, the letters started merging and moving and changing shape until suddenly Poppy realised she could read them.

Hello.

Madame Pearl noticed her concentrating. 'Poppy,' she said, 'can you read what this says?'

Poppy glanced around the class. Everyone was staring at her, waiting to see if she knew the answer. *Here we go*, she thought desperately. *I'll look like a know-it-all again!*

So Poppy shook her head. 'Nope,' she said. 'I have no idea.'

Madame Pearl looked surprised. 'How unusual,' she said, peering closely at Poppy. 'Golden genies are usually very quick to understand Swirl.'

Poppy felt her face go red. Could her teacher tell she was lying? She shrugged, trying to look innocent. 'I guess Golden genies don't know everything,' she said.

To Poppy's relief, Madame Pearl turned back to the class. 'Never mind. Now, Twos,' she said. 'It's time for you to try writing in Swirl. We won't use our jotters today, we'll just write straight into the air.'

'There's just one slight problem with that,' said Jake, holding up his hand. 'My finger has no smoke.'

Madame Pearl's eyes twinkled. 'Of course it does, Jake,' she said. 'You just need to activate the smoke by tapping your wrist twice.'

Jake tapped his wrist sharply and then swooshed his finger through the air. Sure enough, it left a smoky streak. Poppy laughed at Jake's surprised face.

'Not bad,' said Madame Pearl. 'The smoke is a little green, but that will improve. Now, everyone else try.'

Poppy tapped her wrist and did a cautious swish with her pointer finger. Sure enough, bluish smoke began trailing out of her finger. Soon the air was filled with smoky stripes in many different colours.

Once everyone could make smoke, Madame Pearl called the students up to the front one-by-one to try writing the word 'hello'. Most of the class found it very difficult. Sometimes the problem was that the smoke came out of their fingers too quickly or too slowly. Sometimes the letters were too large, or so small that they all squashed together.

When Jake tried, he wrote so slowly that the first few letters had blown away before he'd written the last ones. But it didn't seem to bother him too much. 'I'll just write "hi" next time,' he joked. 'That'll be quicker.'

'Now your turn, Poppy,' said Madame
Pearl. Poppy came out the front and started
to write. The smoke from her finger was not
too fast and not too slow and the letters were
neither too large nor too small.

Her teacher was delighted. 'Perfect, Poppy!'
she said. 'That is the most impressive first
attempt at writing in Swirl I've ever seen. I just
knew you would have natural talent.'

Poppy bit her lip and glanced around
the class. Was everyone thinking she was a

show-off? The other tweenies seemed pretty preoccupied with practising their own Swirl, but Poppy was sure she caught a few of them rolling their eyes.

Then Madame Pearl wrote something else in the air. Poppy could read it easily.

My name is Poppy.

'Try writing this sentence,' her teacher said, patting her on the arm.

Poppy hesitated. It was bad enough that her first attempt had gone perfectly. If she wrote a whole sentence, the other tweenies would *definitely* think she was a know-it-all. So she pulled a worried face, like she wasn't sure she could do it. 'I'll try, Madame Pearl,' she said. 'But it looks hard.'

Poppy started swirling her finger through the air, doing loops and lines. Then she stepped

back. 'How did I go?' she asked, trying to keep a straight face.

Madame Pearl frowned. 'That doesn't look like what I wrote,' she said.

'Hey!' interrupted Jake, laughing. 'It looks like me!'

It was true. Poppy hadn't copied Madame Pearl's sentence at all. She'd drawn a picture of a boy genie's face with a very cheeky smile.

Poppy pretended to be surprised. 'You're right,' she said. 'It does look a bit like you, Jake. But it's not quite right.' Then Poppy gently blew the smoke just a little. The eyes changed shape and suddenly they looked like they were crossed. 'That's better,' she grinned.

The class burst into giggles. Even Madame Pearl was smiling. 'I'm impressed with your drawing skills, Poppy,' she said. 'Drawing with

129

smoke is very hard to do! But then, Golden genies are often brilliant artists.'

Poppy groaned inwardly. 'Thanks, Madame Pearl,' she muttered, and headed back to her cushion. She was *trying* to be ordinary, but somehow she always ended up standing out.

Jake was still laughing about the drawing when the class ended. 'Being Golden has made you naughty,' he said, waggling his finger at her.

Poppy shrugged. 'There's nothing wrong with having some fun occasionally, is there?'

'Of course not,' replied Jake. 'So long as you're *really* having fun and not just trying to make people think you're someone you're not.'

Poppy felt a bit taken aback by that, but before she could say anything, her Dial-Up

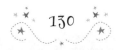

flashed. Poppy's heart did a double thump as she read the message that had appeared.

Bottle Hop starts in ten minutes. Meet
in the Quartz Bottle. Zara.

The message faded and was replaced by another one.

This is my last warning. DON'T DO THE
BOTTLE HOP! Regards, your Dial-Up.

Then it switched itself off with an angry-sounding click.

Chapter 9

Jake read the message over Poppy's shoulder. 'Bottle Hop!' he said. 'So that's what you were up to this morning!'

There was no point denying it, so Poppy told Jake everything she knew about the Bottle Hop. Jake listened with wide eyes.

When she'd finished, he jumped up and grabbed her arm. 'I'm coming for sure!'

Poppy shook her head. 'No, Jake,' she said. 'Zara would *kill* me if I brought you along.

It's supposed to be top secret.'

Jake looked at her sternly. 'There's no way I'm letting you do it on your own, Poppy,' he said. 'Anything might happen. I should be there, for safety's sake.'

Poppy raised an eyebrow. 'I think what you mean is, this sounds like fun and there's no way you're missing out!'

Jake grinned. 'Well, that too,' he admitted. 'Come on, let's *go*.'

'OK,' sighed Poppy. Secretly, she quite liked the idea of Jake coming with her. 'But Zara is *not* going to like this.'

Poppy was right. Zara frowned darkly when she spotted Jake with Poppy in the Quartz Bottle. 'What's he doing here?' she demanded.

'I'm her mechanic,' said Jake politely. 'If Poppy is going to ride that mangy old rug of hers I have to come too. It could fall apart at any moment.'

Rocket was not impressed by Jake's comment. His tassels all stood up like bristles and he angrily swiped at Jake's ankle with one corner. Jake leapt neatly leapt out of the way.

'Nice try, Doormat,' he laughed. 'But waaaay too slow.' Then he looked at Zara. 'So, can I go with Poppy?'

For a moment, Zara didn't reply. She walked over and brushed her hand over Rocket, bending closer to inspect something. Then she shrugged and said, 'It's up to Poppy, I suppose. If she really wants to slow herself down, that's her choice.'

Poppy tugged her carpet out from under

Zara's reach, and Jake nodded eagerly. 'Don't worry,' he said. 'Poppy'll win the race easily. She could probably win it blindfolded.'

Zara raised an eyebrow. 'We'll see about that.'

'OK, racers. Board your rugs,' commanded Louis, who was also there.

Poppy climbed on the front of Rocket and Jake scrambled on the back, carefully avoiding Rocket's tassels, which were whipping at his legs. Poppy pulled out her Location Lamp and ran a finger over the mysterious symbols carved into the lid. She felt a little shiver of excitement through her spine. *I bet none of the other Twos are doing anything like this!* she thought.

'Don't forget your Dial-Up for taking videos of the bottles you visit,' reminded Santino.

'If you don't have proof of visiting a bottle, you won't get any points for it.'

Poppy switched her Dial-Up into video mode, and decided to un-mute it as well. The face did not reappear and Poppy felt a twinge of guilt. *I must have pressed the 'grumpy' profile,* thought Poppy. *It's really cross with me.*

'Hoppers, prepare for flight!' said Louis.

Poppy grabbed hold of her lamp. Which way should she twist it first?

Zara gave Poppy a strange grin. 'Good luck, Goldie.'

Then, just as she twisted the lid of the Location Lamp, Poppy thought she heard Zara mutter something else.

'Because you'll need it!'

As the darkness swirled up around them, Poppy called out, 'Hold tight, Jake!' Then she urged Rocket into flight, although she had no idea which way to head. She just knew that the best way to deal with the strong winds swirling around them was to fly as fast as they could. Finally, the wind dropped away and Poppy slowed Rocket down.

The dark mist around them gradually cleared and Poppy looked around. They were flying over a beautiful, sunny meadow filled with flowers and trees heavy with fruit. The sky was tinged with a deep purple, and Poppy's heart leapt with excitement.

'This must be some sort of old orchard,' she called over her shoulder to Jake. 'I can just imagine the ancient genies coming here on picnics.'

'You're making me hungry! Can you tell the doormat to fly down close to the trees?' said Jake. 'I want to eat some of those cherries. They look delicious.'

Instantly, Rocket whooshed down steeply towards the trees. 'Aaah!' yelled Jake, trying to hold on and cover his head at the same time.

'Rocket,' said Poppy, trying not to laugh. 'Are you trying to scare Jake? Slow down, please.' Her carpet did as she asked, but flipped his tassels in a pleased kind of way.

As they swished past the cherry tree, Poppy took a closer look. The fruit looked very hard and very shiny. Suddenly she realised what they were. 'They're rubies!' she exclaimed.

'You're right!' said Jake, looking around. 'This is a gemstone orchard.'

It was true. The apples were actually enormous emeralds and the oranges were made of smooth, glittering tiger's eyes.

'Let's pick some,' said Jake, his eyes gleaming. 'Just one of those apples would be worth a fortune.'

But Poppy shook her head. 'No,' she said. 'We'd better leave everything as we find it.'

139

No-one had told her that this was a rule, but it just didn't seem right to take anything from such a beautiful, ancient place.

Poppy flew down low over the orchard, taking a video with her Dial-Up. She could have stayed in the orchard forever. But they had a race to win!

'OK, next stop,' she said, pulling out her Location Lamp and twisting the lid to a new symbol. There was a clap of thunder, and suddenly Poppy and Jake found themselves flying through a whole new bottle.

The new world looked like the inside of a winter snow dome, except that it had the same purple light they'd found in the orchard bottle. There were small fir trees, covered in the white, powdery snow. Little candles were balanced on the tip of each branch, burning

not only in gold, but in blue, red, purple and green. There was a faint sound of bells in the air, which Poppy realised was coming from the tiny silver birds flying around.

'It's like a fairytale, isn't it?' said Poppy, as a soft dusting of snow fell over the carpet and on their heads. She stuck out her tongue to catch a snowflake, and realised what it was. 'Sugar!'

'I wonder what the ancient genies used this place for?' said Jake, tilting his head back to lick the air.

'Maybe they used to come here for their parties,' suggested Poppy. 'Or maybe it belonged to a genie who loved snow.'

'And sugar,' Jake added.

'Exactly,' laughed Poppy. 'Come on, let's go for a zoom. Hold on!'

Rocket took off joyfully, skimming low over the fir trees so that the coloured flames of the candles trembled in the breeze. It felt wonderful to fly so fast, even though Jake was yelling at her to slow down!

So this is what Bottle Hopping is all about, thought Poppy. She felt a stab of disappointment when she saw the curve of the bottle's wall looming up ahead. But then again, maybe the next bottle would be even better.

'Time to hop again,' she called to Jake. She twisted the lid to a new symbol, and a moment later the sugary snow disappeared.

The next bottle contained a dense forest, with trees so tall that Poppy couldn't see the ground at all as they sailed over the canopy. Strange, beautiful

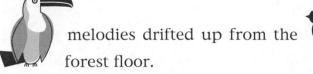

melodies drifted up from the forest floor.

Poppy pointed Rocket downwards and started weaving expertly in and out of the trees. Soon, Poppy and Jake spotted unusual-looking birds flittering through the foliage. 'I think we're in some kind of old aviary,' said Poppy. Some of the birds were no bigger than a coin, with brightly glittering wings, while others were as large as ponies, with loud cries that shook the leaves.

'Aren't they beautiful?' whispered Poppy.

A bird with rainbow-coloured wings landed beside them on the carpet. Poppy started filming it with her Dial-Up. The bird fanned its tail feathers, which were all the colours of the rainbow.

'I'd love to have one of those feathers,' said Jake, reaching out a hand.

'Jake!' exclaimed Poppy. 'Don't you dare!' The bird gave Jake an offended look and then flew off, doing several impressive loops before disappearing into the forest.

Poppy looked at her watch. 'I think we've got time to visit one more bottle before our twenty minutes are up,' she said. 'What do you think? Shall we do it?'

But just then there was a low rumbling noise. Poppy looked around. Menacing storm clouds had formed at the top of the bottle, and thunder was beginning to growl.

'That doesn't look good,' said Poppy, frowning. 'It's like a storm is brewing.'

'Really?' said Jake, looking around

144

nervously. 'I didn't realise you could have storms in genie bottles.'

'Me neither,' Poppy said, slowly. She had a bad feeling in the pit of her stomach, even though she didn't know why. 'Maybe it's a protection charm trying to get rid of us, like the ones my Dial-Up warned me about.' Poppy suddenly missed her Dial-Up's chattiness. It would have been useful in this situation.

There was nothing for it but to get out of there as quickly as possible. Poppy reached for her Location Lamp and pressed down on the lid so they could go back to the Quartz Bottle. But the lid refused to move.

Uh-oh, thought Poppy, her throat suddenly dry. Then there was a boom of thunder and a flash of light. A heavy wind began buffeting Rocket from side to side.

'Poppy,' said Jake, his voice a little shaky. 'We're heading right for the storm.'

'Don't worry, Jake,' said Poppy, keeping her voice calm, although she was feeling scared too. 'We'll be fine.' Then she pressed her hand against Rocket.

'Turn around, Rocket,' Poppy said in a firm voice. They needed to get as far away from the storm as possible, and quickly. But to Poppy's surprise, Rocket didn't turn around. Instead, he did something very odd. First he started twitching all over. Then he did an enormous shiver and leapt forwards – heading straight for the storm instead of away from it!

'This is bad, Poppy,' yelled Jake. '*Very* bad.'

'It's under control,' Poppy called back. 'I'll get us out of here in just a sec.' She hoped the wind would disguise the panic in her voice.

With one hand, Poppy tried to steer her out-of-control rug away from the storm, and with the other she tried to turn the stuck lid of the Location Lamp. The sky was growing darker.

Desperately, Poppy pressed down on the Location Lamp lid again. 'Listen, lid,' she muttered. 'If you don't do what I'm asking, I'm going to throw you off the carpet.'

A second later, there was a little popping noise, and finally the lid clicked into place. But the black clouds had surrounded them, and the wind spun Rocket around in a spiral.

'I'm slipping off!' yelled Jake, scrambling on the carpet behind her. Poppy grabbed Jake's arm and pulled him back onto the rug just as the last of the light disappeared and Rocket plummeted downwards.

Chapter 10

Suddenly, everything fell silent. *The wind has gone*, Poppy thought. And then she realised that although her body still *felt* like it was doing crazy cartwheels through space, she was now lying on firm ground.

When Poppy opened her eyes, she saw that the sky was no longer purple, but a dusty yellow. Relief flooded through her. *We're back in the Quartz Bottle*, she thought. She blinked a few times, and found herself surrounded by

anxious-looking Bottle Hoppers.

'You're OK,' said Santino in a low voice. 'We were getting worried. You've been gone for ages.'

He was standing next to Zara, who looked every bit as relieved as the others – maybe even more so. 'It's ... it's good that you're back,' Zara said quietly. There was a strange expression on her face.

Poppy gazed at her mentor for a moment, still feeling a bit light-headed. Then she remembered her friend. 'Jake,' she said, sitting bolt upright. 'Is Jake here?'

'I'm right behind you,' said a voice. Poppy turned and sure enough, there he was. And apart from being very windswept, he looked fine.

'I'm so glad to see you!' cried Poppy, flinging her arms around him.

Jake shrugged her off, embarrassed. 'Stop that,' he muttered. 'Everyone will think we love each other or something.'

'What happened to you guys?' asked Santino.

'We got caught in a storm,' said Jake, with a grin. 'It was so awesome. Poppy nearly fell off and I had to rescue her.'

Poppy raised her eyebrows. 'Excuse me? Who saved *who*?'

Jake grinned. 'Well, close enough,' he said cheekily.

'So now that we know everyone is OK,' said Santino, his usual smile returning to his face, 'let's watch the videos of the bottles you guys visited. Zara, you go first. How many bottles did you visit?'

'I think it was three,' said Zara in a small

voice. She pulled out her Dial-Up.

Jake nudged Poppy. 'Zara obviously went to some totally dud bottles – you can tell from her face,' he whispered. 'That means we might win, even though it's a tie!'

Poppy nodded. Her mentor seemed very quiet and subdued for once. *I would've thought she'd be boasting about how many great bottles she visited*, thought Poppy. It was almost like Zara didn't care about the Bottle Hop anymore.

DID YOU KNOW?

In a tie-break situation, the other Bottle Hoppers will vote on the winner based on who they think has visited the most interesting or dangerous bottles.

Zara played the video of the first bottle she visited. Poppy gasped. It was a beautiful castle – perfectly preserved in the ancient bottle.

'It's amazing,' she said. 'It's like a king and queen are still living there.'

But Zara didn't seem at all interested in the clip. She clicked through wordlessly to the next bottle.

'Is that an old lolly shop?' asked Jake, leaning forward.

Zara nodded. 'It had some amazing-looking lollies.'

'I wish *we'd* found that bottle,' Jake said, wistfully.

Poppy laughed. 'Those lollies would've been centuries old,' she pointed out. 'They would taste terrible.'

'They look fine to me,' said Jake.

153

Zara's final video seemed to be of a vast desert. 'Why is the sand so shiny?' someone asked.

'That's not sand,' said Zara. 'It's gold dust.'

Jake's mouth dropped open. 'Did you scoop any of it up?'

'Of course she didn't!' said Santino. 'If you take anything from one of those old bottles – even a single grain of sand – you risk setting off an ancient protection charm. Those charms can be really powerful, like the most massive storm you've ever seen.'

'Oh,' said Jake, looking strange. 'Even one grain of sand, huh?' He suddenly seemed nervous.

An unpleasant thought crept into Poppy's head. 'Jake,' she said, frowning a little at him.

Jake shifted uncomfortably. 'What?'

'Did you take a tail feather from that bird in the aviary world?' asked Poppy. Jake's face went red.

'I didn't pull it out,' he said defensively. 'The bird dropped one on the carpet when it flew off. I figured it was a present so I popped it in my pocket.'

DID YOU KNOW?

Ancient genies protected their bottles from intruders by placing protection charms on them. Some charms are very mild and just make the intruding genie feel itchy. Others are stronger and can cause the whole bottle to plunge into darkness, or start spinning wildly. Most protection charms only kick into action if something is taken from the bottle.

Poppy groaned. 'Why would you do something like that, especially after I said we shouldn't take anything?'

Jake looked sheepish. 'I'm sorry. I thought you were being a ...' His voice trailed off.

'A *goody-goody?*' asked Poppy crossly, and Jake nodded. 'It was a really dumb thing to do, Jake,' said Poppy. 'It's probably the reason why Rocket was acting so strangely too.'

Santino looked puzzled. 'I've never heard of a protection charm affecting a carpet before,' he said. 'What happened exactly?'

Poppy described Rocket's unusual behaviour.

When she'd finished, Santino frowned and bent down to examine Rocket. A moment later he looked up. 'Just what I thought,' he said. 'Look at this.'

Poppy looked where he was pointing. Sprinkled through Rocket's tassels was a fine white powder. 'That's just snow from one of the bottles we visited,' said Jake.

But Santino shook his head. 'That's not snow,' he said. 'That's Go Fast spray. You know, the opposite of Go Slow spray. It's used to make magic carpets go much faster than they normally would. If you put too much on, it can make the carpet go out of control. It's totally banned at Genie High.'

the spray is banned in most genie high schools

even a small squirt of Go Fast spray makes magic carpets fly very quickly

go fast

'But how would that have gotten on Rocket?' asked Poppy, confused.

Santino folded his arms. 'Someone tried to sabotage your Bottle Hop, Poppy,' he said bluntly.

'Who would *do* that?' asked Poppy. Even as she said it, she realised there was only one possible answer. Poppy spun around to face Zara. Her mentor was staring at the ground, her face pale.

'Zara, was it you?' Poppy asked, her heart pounding. For a moment, Zara stood very still. Then she nodded slowly. All the Bottle Hoppers gasped in dismay.

'Zara,' said Santino, shaking his head. 'How could you?'

'It was meant to be joke,' Zara said softly. 'I didn't think it would cause so much trouble.'

'Some joke,' Poppy snapped, her anger bubbling over. 'Jake and I could have been seriously hurt!'

'I can't believe you'd do something so nasty just to win a race,' said Santino, frowning. 'And so dangerous too! Why did you put so *much* spray on Rocket?'

Zara looked even more ashamed. 'Because when I sprayed a small amount on the first time, Poppy didn't even seem to notice,' she said in a tiny voice. 'So I thought it would be OK to add a bit more this time.'

Poppy stared at Zara, horrified. 'You've done this *before*?'

'Yes,' admitted Zara. 'Remember your first day in the Velodrome Bottle when your beginner rug went mad? I sprayed *that* carpet because I thought it'd

be funny to see you fall off. But you didn't.'

'What a terrible thing to do, Zara,' said Jake, disgusted. 'You should be disqualified from the Bottle Hop.'

Santino nodded. 'I agree,' he said, his face hard. 'I never thought you'd do something like this. You should be disqualified from the whole *club*.'

'No!' cried Zara. She grabbed Poppy's shoulder. 'Poppy, I'm so sorry for what I did. And I'm sorry for being such a terrible mentor too. I know it was mean to put Go Fast spray on your carpet. I didn't think anything bad would happen. I've been so dumb! *Please* forgive me.'

'Don't forgive her, Poppy,' said Jake, still sounding furious. 'Why should you?'

Poppy hesitated. She was angry with Zara.

Really angry. And besides that, her feelings were hurt.

'Why do you hate me so much, Zara?' Poppy asked. 'Is it because I'm a Golden genie?'

Zara sighed. 'Everyone was so excited about you coming to Genie High. I suppose I wondered what all the fuss was about. And I decided that I wasn't going to be dazzled by you.' Looking upset, Zara sank down on the floor right near Rocket. Suddenly, a strange expression came over her face, and she reached out a hand towards the carpet.

'Don't touch Rocket!' snapped Poppy.

But Zara peered even closer at the carpet, her face turning white. 'Poppy,' she said, 'I know you're angry with me, but this is serious. I think – I think Rocket might be sick.'

'Don't try and trick me, Zara,' Poppy said.

Zara shook her head. 'I'm not tricking,' she said. 'Look. He's started to fade. That's a really bad thing in a carpet. It means that his magic's starting to drain out.'

Poppy examined Rocket closely, but she couldn't see what Zara was talking about. Was this just another mean stunt?

Then Santino came up beside her. 'Poppy,' he said urgently. 'I know you don't trust Zara

right now and I don't blame you. But you should listen to her on this. She knows a lot about magic carpets and she wouldn't joke about Rocket.'

Zara nodded. 'I'm not messing around,' she said. 'Rocket needs to see a repairer. Unfortunately there's only one repairer good enough for a job like this, and you won't want to hear who that is.'

'Just tell me, Zara,' said Poppy, feeling frustrated.

Zara swallowed. 'It's Lady Topaz.'

Chapter 11

Everyone fell silent. Poppy stared at Zara, not knowing what to say. Lady Topaz was the last person she wanted to run into right now! She was bound to ask questions about what Poppy had been doing with Rocket.

'It's a trick, Poppy,' growled Jake. 'You'll end up being expelled.'

'Can't you fix him, Zara?' asked Poppy. But in her heart she knew that she would have to find Lady Topaz.

Zara looked at Poppy and shook her head. Her eyes were very serious. 'Rug repairing is an ancient art, and hardly anyone can do it. I can promise you two things. The first is that Lady Topaz is the best genie to fix Rocket. If we don't go to her, then Rocket might fade away to nothing.'

Poppy imagined Rocket disappearing and felt a lump in her throat. Even being expelled from Genie High would be better than that.

'What's the other promise?' Poppy asked.

'I'll come with you to see Lady Topaz,' said Zara. 'So if she expels you, she'll expel me too.'

'You would really do that?' said Poppy.

'Yes,' nodded Zara. 'I owe you that much. But we need to get going. Rocket won't last much longer.'

Poppy's mind whirled. She still didn't trust Zara, but it meant a lot that she was prepared to come with her.

'OK, let's go,' she said, bending down to gather up her carpet. Rocket seemed very floppy and Poppy could see now that he was indeed losing colour. It was awful.

Zara gave her a sympathetic look, then unrolled her own carpet and jumped on.

'Wait,' said Jake, as Poppy stepped gingerly onto Zara's carpet. 'How do you even know where to find Lady Topaz? She could be anywhere in the school. It's not like her personal genie bottle is listed on our Dial-Up.'

'It's true that Lady Topaz could be anywhere,' admitted Zara, settling in, 'but I know where her bottle is. We may as well start there. And we won't be using our Dial-Ups to

166

find it.' She pulled out her Location Lamp.

'Zara, you still have the ancient lid on the top,' said Poppy. 'Aren't we going to find Lady Topaz?'

Zara nodded. 'Hold on tight.' She twisted the dial and soon they were surrounded by smoke.

When the smoke cleared, Poppy knew from the sky's purplish tinge that they were back in one of the ancient bottles. They seemed to be in the middle of a dark, dense wood.

Zara expertly guided her carpet in and out of the trees. Poppy had the feeling they were trying to grab at her with their branches. *It's just my imagination,* she told herself. All the

same, she held on to Rocket extra-tight.

'How is Rocket doing?' asked Zara.

'He's fading fast,' replied Poppy nervously, stroking her carpet. 'Even his tassels look sick.'

Zara urged her carpet on even faster than before. Poppy couldn't understand how she was managing to avoid the trees. But Zara didn't even come close to hitting one. She was definitely an expert flyer. 'Hold on,' said Zara suddenly, 'we're going down.'

The ground started rushing up towards them. *We're going to crash!* thought Poppy.

But instead, Zara guided her carpet down into what looked like a giant rabbit tunnel. Inside it was pitch black. 'We're almost there now,' she called back.

A second later, Poppy could see a faint glow up ahead. As the light grew stronger,

168

Zara slowed her carpet down, and finally came to land gently on the ground.

Still clutching Rocket tightly, Poppy stood up and looked around. They were in a vast underground workshop. Wool in every colour imaginable (and some colours Poppy had never seen before) hung from hooks on the ceiling. There were hundreds of carpets stacked up in piles everywhere. In the middle of the room was a giant wooden table, covered with needles of all different shapes and sizes, and more scissors than Poppy had ever seen.

'Wow,' said Poppy, looking around. 'How did you know this was here?'

'I stumbled upon it once during a Bottle Hop,' replied Zara. 'I realised it was Lady Topaz's bottle when I saw the chairs.' Sure enough, around the table were chairs with

lions' feet, just like the one Lady Topaz had sat on during their first Carpet Control lesson. 'Luckily Lady Topaz wasn't in it at the time, so she didn't see me.'

'There's something I don't get,' said Poppy. 'How come Lady Topaz has an ancient bottle?'

'Because she's an ancient genie,' said Zara.

'Santino wasn't kidding when he said she'd been the principal for a thousand years.'

'Lady Topaz is ancient?' said Poppy in disbelief. 'She can't be. She looks so young!'

'Oh, I'm definitely *ancient*,' said a deep, rich voice. There was a puff of purple smoke, and when it cleared, Lady Topaz was standing in the middle of the workshop.

She came up beside Poppy and gave Rocket a gentle stroke. 'How are you, Knotty?' she said, a note of anxiety creeping into her warm voice.

'Knotty?' asked Poppy.

'Yes, this is Knotty,' said Lady Topaz, peering closely. 'Or at least he was, back when I first made him.'

Poppy stared at Lady Topaz, her mouth hanging open. She knew it was rude, but she

couldn't help it. 'You made Rocket?'

'Oh yes. It was many years ago now. He's been handed down from Golden genie to Golden genie ever since, lovely old fellow.'

'But Lexie – er, I mean, Princess Alexandria gave him to me,' said Poppy, puzzled.

'Yes, indeed,' said Lady Topaz, 'Princess Alexandria is a Golden genie too. As are all the genies who have owned this carpet, including myself.'

'You're a Golden genie too?' said Poppy, astonished.

'Certainly. And I excelled at carpet making,' said Lady Topaz. 'Knotty was my best carpet. He's not just any old rug. He's always been passed on to someone deserving.' Then her voice became stern. 'I'm very disappointed to see him like this, Poppy. Are you going to tell

172

me what has happened?'

'He was injured during a Bottle Hop,' said Poppy, near tears. 'Can you fix him?'

Lady Topaz looked at Poppy severely. 'You do realise that Bottle Hops are strictly forbidden at Genie High?'

Poppy nodded miserably. 'I know. But can you help him?'

Lady Topaz took Rocket and laid him out on the workbench. 'Yes, this is very serious,' she muttered. 'He's lost a lot of colour. Zara, please pass me the absorption paper. It's that big roll on the shelf behind me. Quickly!'

Zara ran over to the jumbled shelves behind Lady Topaz and pulled out what looked like a large roll of tracing paper. She handed it to Lady Topaz, who expertly tore off a length and lay it down over Rocket.

The paper turned into a sparkling, golden liquid that seeped into Rocket's surface.

'The colours look brighter already,' said Poppy.

'Yes, it's helped,' agreed Lady Topaz. 'But it's not over yet. This rip needs repairing.' She pointed to a small hole. 'This is where the colour is seeping from.' She clicked her fingers and a golden needle with a small pair of fluttering wings swooped over. Lady Topaz threaded it expertly with the finest golden thread that Poppy had ever seen. Then she began to sew.

Rocket twitched as the needle went into him and Poppy winced to see it. Poor Rocket!

Poppy hardly dared to breathe while Lady Topaz worked. The thread seemed so fine. How could it possibly keep Rocket together? Poppy

kept patting Rocket and hoping everything would be OK. Zara looked just as worried as Poppy felt.

Finally, Lady Topaz picked up a tiny pair of golden scissors and cut the thread. Then she sat back.

Poppy looked at her anxiously. 'Is Rocket going to be OK now?'

Lady Topaz sighed and shook her head. 'It's too early to say,' she replied. 'We need to wait for a few minutes to see how he responds to the mending. The rip was caused by ancient magic, and this makes the injury difficult to repair. The other problem is Rocket's age, which makes him very fragile. And, of course, he's a story rug, which complicates things even more. All the threads must match up perfectly or the story won't make any sense.'

'What do you mean, a story rug?' asked Poppy.

'It means the patterns on the carpet aren't just for decoration,' explained Lady Topaz, pointing to the curly looping patterns covering Rocket. 'They can be read, like a story.'

At first Poppy had no idea what Lady Topaz was talking about. But then she realised that Rocket's markings looked familiar. 'It's Swirl,' she murmured.

'That's right,' said Lady Topaz. 'Can you understand what it says?'

Poppy started to read out loud. *'Topaz thought she was just an ordinary girl …'* She stopped, amazed. 'Is this story about you?'

'In a way,' said Lady Topaz. 'I made the carpet, so the story begins with me. But it goes on to tell the story of all the Golden

genies who have owned the rug.' She pointed to a squiggle. 'This is where you found the genie bottle on your twelfth birthday. And over here is where you didn't hide your bottle properly and your sister found it.'

Poppy pulled a face. 'So it's got the bad stuff as well as the good stuff then?' she said.

Lady Topaz nodded. 'It has everything.'

Zara pointed to part of the design that looked like the pattern had trailed away to nothing. 'What's this?' she said.

'That's what's happening right now,' said Lady Topaz. 'While we wait to see whether Rocket will get better.'

The three genies sat there in silence, watching and waiting. Poppy felt like she might explode from nervousness.

Then suddenly, Rocket's tassels twitched

slightly. A moment later, they twitched again, more strongly this time. Poppy's heart beat wildly against her rib cage.

Then there was a whooshing noise and Rocket up flew off the table and raced around the room doing wild loops. 'Rocket!' yelled Poppy. 'You're fixed!'

'Stop showing off, Knotty,' said Lady Topaz with a smile. Rocket slowed down, then leapt into Poppy's arms and nuzzled in.

'That carpet pretends to be invincible,' warned Lady Topaz, 'but he's not. Make sure he takes it easy.'

Poppy nodded. 'I will,' she promised.

'And now that Rocket is better,' said Lady Topaz, 'why don't we talk about your punishment?'

Chapter 12

'Lady Topaz,' said Zara quickly. 'None of this is Poppy's fault. I talked her into doing the Bottle Hop. She would've been way too scared to do it otherwise.'

Poppy stared at Zara. Was it possible she was being genuinely nice? Then she realised what Zara had actually said. 'Hang on a minute,' Poppy said hotly. 'I was *not* too scared. But I should've been trying to talk you *out* of racing, not joining in myself.'

Zara rolled her eyes. 'Don't get all Golden on me and try to take the blame, Poppy,' she said, shooting her a look. 'If anyone's getting expelled it should be me.'

'Girls, please,' said Lady Topaz, putting up her hand. She looked like she was trying to suppress a smile. 'There are enough punishments to go around.' Then her stern expression returned. 'I *should* expel you both. Zara, you're supposed to be Poppy's mentor. What kind of mentor talks her Two into doing something as dangerous as a Bottle Hop?'

Zara flushed bright red. Lady Topaz turned to Poppy. 'And you, Poppy, should have known better. Golden genies are supposed to set a good example. Even worse, you almost lost Rocket – an ancient and valuable story rug. If he had faded away, all his knowledge

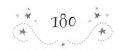

and wisdom would have been lost. I don't understand why you would do such a thing.'

Poppy felt awful. Everything Lady Topaz was saying was true, but it was terrible to hear it spoken out loud like this. She glanced at Zara, who had gone pale.

'But,' said Lady Topaz, 'I am not going to expel either of you.'

Poppy stared up at her, not sure she'd heard correctly. 'You're not going to expel us?'

Lady Topaz shook her head. 'No,' she said. 'However, this is a serious matter, and you will each be given three punishments.' She paused, looking each girl in the eye. 'First, you will each be suspended from Genie High for three days. During this time you will not be allowed into the Genie Realm. That should

181

give you time to think about your actions.'

Poppy was horrified. Three whole days out of the Genie Realm!

'You deliberately disobeyed the school rules,' Lady Topaz continued, 'and there is just one reason you are not being expelled. Do you know what that is?'

Both Poppy and Zara looked at their feet.

'It's because you showed a great deal of bravery coming to find me,' said Lady Topaz, her voice suddenly gentle. 'You knew that you risked getting into a lot of trouble by bringing Rocket to me. But you did it anyway. And that shows exactly the sort of qualities I'd expect to see in a mentor and a Golden genie. So I'm giving you both another chance.'

Zara and Poppy both looked up and smiled. They couldn't believe their luck.

'Thank you, Lady Topaz,' said Zara quietly.
'But somehow I don't think Poppy is going to
want me to be her mentor after this.'

Poppy shook her head. 'Actually,' she
said to Zara with a shy smile, 'you're wrong.
I mean, I *did* feel like that. And OK, so you
haven't been the friendliest mentor so far. But
you saved Rocket and that was really brave.

So how about we give it another go?'

Zara beamed, the colour returning to her cheeks. 'Really?'

Poppy nodded. 'But could you just forget about me being a Golden genie? It'll make things a lot easier.'

'Tell me,' said Lady Topaz, turning her piercingly blue eyes to Poppy. 'Do you enjoy being Golden?'

Poppy hesitated. No-one had ever asked her if she enjoyed it before. She thought it was just something she was and she didn't have much say in it. But there was something in Lady Topaz's voice that made her feel that she could speak the truth.

'I hate it,' Poppy blurted. 'Genie High has been really fun so far. But it would be so much *more* fun if I was just a normal tweenie.

Everyone expects me to be some super student who knows everything without being taught. Or even worse, they think I'm a goody-goody and that I'm going to dob on them all the time.'

Lady Topaz put her head on one side. 'What do you think being a Golden genie means?'

Poppy thought for a moment, then shook her head. 'I don't know,' she admitted. 'It doesn't mean I'm the best at everything. And it doesn't mean that I don't make mistakes, because I still make heaps of them. I don't think I'm all that special. I just feel ordinary.' Then Poppy looked at Lady Topaz hopefully. 'What *does* it mean?'

Lady Topaz smiled. 'You're right, Poppy. Being a Golden genie doesn't make you better

than anyone else. What makes you a Golden genie is that you have a good heart. You see, Golden genies have a heart of gold.'

Zara looked at Poppy with surprise. 'But I always thought Golden genies were supposed to have special talents,' said Zara.

'We all have special talents,' laughed Lady Topaz. 'We're genies, after all. If you hadn't noticed what was happening to Poppy's carpet, Zara, it might have faded entirely. And that would have been terrible. You used your special talent with carpets to save Rocket.'

Poppy's mind started ticking over. 'But if everyone has special talents, why do we need Golden genies?' she asked.

'The Genie Realm is full of riches, Poppy. Genies could easily be very greedy and selfish,' said Lady Topaz. 'Golden genies are

important because their good hearts help them to make the right decisions and they set an example for others.'

'I didn't make the right decision about Bottle Hopping,' said Poppy, realising how silly she had been.

'Ah yes, thank you for reminding me,' said Lady Topaz, 'I had not quite finished with your punishments.' Poppy prepared herself for the worst. 'The second punishment is that when you come back to Genie High, you will both spend every Monday afternoon in my Workshop Bottle. I will teach you about rug repairing.'

Poppy glanced at Lady Topaz in surprise. That didn't seem like a very bad punishment. She was expecting that she'd have to clean bins or something.

187

But Zara bit her lip. 'Lady Topaz?' she asked. 'Does it have to be Monday afternoon? That's when my Extreme Flying class is on.'

Lady Topaz nodded. 'Yes, I know,' she said. 'Which leads me to the third part of your punishment. Absolutely no riding for either of you for three months.'

Poppy stared at her in horror. 'But I can't go that long without riding!'

'Well, you will have to,' said Lady Topaz firmly. 'Besides, Rocket needs time to recover from his injury. It won't do you any harm to have a break. You are already a long way ahead of the other Twos. It will give them a chance to catch up with you. Does that sound fair?'

Zara and Poppy looked at each other, then nodded. It was going to be horrible, not being able to ride. And it was going to be even worse,

having to spend three days away from Genie High. But at least they hadn't been expelled.

Then Lady Topaz looked at her watch. 'You should head back to school now to pack up your things. I'm sure the other Bottle Hoppers are curious to know how you are going. You'd also better break the news to them that the Bottle Hops are officially over. As you have seen today, visiting ancient bottles can be extremely dangerous. However, perhaps in future we will organise a school excursion when you can visit some of the ancient bottles under proper supervision.'

Poppy grinned. That sounded great!

Then Lady Topaz cleared her throat. 'Oh, and Poppy? Tell Jake that he needs to write *I must not go on Bottle Hops* two hundred times. In perfect Swirl.'

Poppy froze. How did Lady Topaz know that Jake had gone too? She'd been very careful not to mention his name.

Lady Topaz seemed to know what Poppy was thinking. 'I received a Dial-Up message that filled me in on everything,' she said.

'You mean you knew about Rocket being injured before we got here?' asked Zara. 'I can't believe one of the Bottle Hoppers blabbed!'

'The message wasn't sent by a genie,' said Lady Topaz. 'The Dial-Up sent it all by itself.'

Poppy was puzzled, until she realised what that meant. She reached into her bag and pulled out her Dial-Up. The little face had reappeared. It looked nervous. Then a message flashed up on the screen.

'You can talk, you know,' said Poppy. 'I un-muted you ages ago.'

190

sorry

The Dial-Up gave a little nervous cough. 'I only told Lady Topaz because I was worried about you,' it said. 'It's my job as a Dial-Up to protect you. When you wouldn't listen to me, I thought I'd better tell Lady Topaz instead.'

'I'm sorry about muting you,' said Poppy. 'It was really mean of me. I could have used your help, too.'

'Oh,' said the Dial-Up, sounding surprised. 'Oh most Magnificent and Magical...' the Dial-Up started to gush.

Poppy shook her head. 'Let's do something we should have done ages ago,' she said, flicking through the voice profile menu. One option caught her eye straight away, and she smiled as she selected it.

'Let's go girls,' said Lady Topaz briskly. 'It's getting late.'

Poppy nodded eagerly. 'I can't wait to get back.' She had so much to tell Jake and the others. *But how am I going to survive three whole days away?* she thought.

'It's good to see you're settling into school, Poppy,' said Lady Topaz. 'It seemed at first

that you had some trouble fitting in.'

'Poppy fits in fine,' Zara butted in. 'I just wish she'd stop boasting about being a Golden genie all the time.'

'I do *not* boast about it!' Poppy said.

'Just teasing, Goldie,' laughed Zara. 'You know I'm here to look after you.'

'I can look after myself, thanks,' said Poppy, but she caught Zara's eye and gave her a friendly wink.

Chapter 13

When Poppy and Zara arrived back at Genie High, they found all the Bottle Hoppers at the Pool Bottle having a swim.

Magic carpets hovered around the outside of the pool with drinks and ice-creams. The ice-creams were studded with small sweets that glittered like jewels, and the drinks had ice cubes that were shaped like shells and fish.

When the Bottle Hoppers saw Poppy and

Zara they rushed over to greet them.

'How did it go?' asked Santino urgently. 'Is Rocket going to be OK?'

Zara and Poppy explained what had happened.

'You're suspended for three days? That's terrible!' said Jake. 'Who would have thought that old doormat could get you in so much trouble?'

Rocket slapped a tassle against Jake's leg.

195

'Watch it,' said Poppy. 'He may be sick but he's still faster than you.'

Poppy looked around the pool, and wished she didn't have to go home.

But leaving the pool party wasn't the only reason Poppy was reluctant to leave. She had just remembered her 'perfect' mum, no doubt waiting to pounce on her as soon as she walked in the door. Not to mention the bird-eating spider wandering around her bedroom.

When Poppy finally returned home, she was more than a little nervous walking into the lounge room. She saw her mum lying on the couch, a pile of paperwork on one side and some dirty laundry on the other. Astrid was sitting on another chair, doing homework with

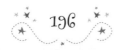

her headphones on. She didn't even look up when Poppy came in.

'Hi, Mum,' said Poppy carefully.

'Hi, sweetie,' her mum replied with a yawn. 'I'm going to make something special for dinner tonight because Dad is coming home. But grab yourself a snack if you're hungry. Not ice-cream though, please!'

'That's OK,' said Poppy hastily. 'I'm not that into ice-cream right now.' She walked to the kitchen, a little confused. Her mum was clearly back to normal. But how had that happened without her making a wish?

In her bag, her Dial-Up beeped. Poppy pulled it out. 'As a special favour, I took the liberty of reversing the wish on your behalf,' the Dial-Up explained quietly. 'I'm allowed to do that in very special circumstances, and it

seemed like you'd had a long day.'

Poppy rushed to check the freezer. Sure enough, the enormous bucket of ice-cream had been pushed to the back, and in front of it were packets of frozen peas and spinach. 'What about the spider?' whispered Poppy nervously.

'Your mum took Bertha back to the pet shop this afternoon,' replied the Dial-Up.

'Phew!' said Poppy. 'Thanks, Dial-Up.'

The Dial-Up winked. 'No problem.'

Poppy grabbed an apple from the fruit bowl, feeling enormously relieved. 'Incredibly helpful' was turning out to be the perfect profile for her Dial-Up.

When Poppy returned to the lounge room, her mum had almost fallen asleep holding a pen in one hand and a shirt in the other.

Poppy suddenly felt very sorry for her mum. *She totally wasted her first two wishes,* she thought. *And she'll probably waste the last one wishing for an early night or something really boring.*

Poppy thought hard. *Maybe I'll try a spot more wish leading. But this time I'll help her wish for something nice.*

'Hey, Mum,' said Poppy, snuggling up beside her on the sofa. 'If a genie suddenly popped up right now and granted you one wish, what would you wish for? But it has to be something just for *you*. No wishing for World Peace or anything like that.'

Her mum yawned and gave her a sleepy grin. 'Why not? World Peace is a lovely thing to wish for.'

Poppy patted her mum on the shoulder.

'I think the genie might find that a bit too complicated,' she explained. 'Especially if it was a beginner genie. So just make a wish for you.'

Poppy's mum thought for a moment. 'Well, right now I wish I could spend a few days on a tropical island,' she said. 'Somewhere I could sit on a beach and drink juice out of a coconut shell.'

Poppy nodded slowly. 'That sounds like a great wish, Mum.'

She closed her eyes and concentrated very carefully on her mother's wish. Then she said the magic word.

When she opened her eyes, she somehow knew that wish had worked.

A few minutes later, the phone rang. Poppy's mum answered it.

'You must have the wrong number,' she

200

said first. Then, as she listened, a strange expression came over her face.

'If this is a joke ...' she began. But her look gradually changed from a suspicious one to a happy one. Then the happy look grew and grew, until Poppy's mum was beaming. 'Thank you,' she said finally. 'Thank you so much!'

'What's happened, Mum?' said Poppy.

Her mum shook her head, like she couldn't quite believe what had just happened. 'It's ridiculous, but according to that person on the phone I've won a holiday for three nights. On a tropical island. At first I didn't think it could be real,' she said. 'But then I remembered I did enter a raffle at the supermarket the other week.'

Poppy jumped up and hugged her mum. 'That's so great,' she said. 'You totally deserve it.'

'It's just so strange, don't you think?' beamed her mum. 'We were just talking about wishes. It's such a coincidence.'

'It *is* kind of weird, I guess,' said Poppy. 'But coincidences happen all the time, Mum.'

Astrid took off her headphones. 'What are

you two talking about?' she asked.

'Mum just won a supermarket raffle!' said Poppy. 'Isn't that amazing? She's going on a holiday to a tropical island.'

Astrid scowled. 'I don't believe it,' she said. 'No-one ever wins those raffles.'

'Yes they do,' Poppy retorted. 'Because Mum just did.'

'A limousine is going to pick me up first thing tomorrow,' announced Mrs Miller. 'I'd better go and pack.'

'Good idea,' said Poppy. 'And don't worry about anything here. Me and Astrid and Dad will be fine. We'll tidy the place up while you're gone.'

'Well,' smiled her mum before she danced off down the hall, 'that would be another wish come true!'

Poppy felt great. Granting a wish – the right kind of wish – was wonderful. But Astrid didn't seem quite so pleased about it all. She frowned at Poppy. 'There is something weird going on,' she said. 'First *you* get a scholarship to an ultra-gifted school. Then mum wins a holiday. But *I* haven't won anything for weeks. It's all wrong.'

'I'm sure you'll have some good luck again soon, sis,' said Poppy cheerfully.

Astrid looked like she had more to say, but just then Poppy's Dial-Up started beeping. 'Sorry,' said Poppy. 'I have to take this call.'

'You've got a *phone*?' said Astrid.

'It's a *school* phone,' said Poppy. 'We ultra-gifted students need them.' Then she slipped off to her room and answered the call. It was Lexie.

'I'm just ringing to see how you're enjoying yourself,' she said. 'I remember my first few days at Genie High. There was so much to get used to. And it's extra-tricky when you're a Golden genie, of course.'

Poppy paused for a moment, thinking about everything that had happened. There had been some hard bits, but there had been plenty of amazing, fun bits too. And it was going to be tough not flying Rocket for three months, but it didn't mean she would enjoy Genie High any less.

'I love Genie High,' said Poppy simply. 'There's nowhere else I'd rather be.'

the end

Follow Elly the **FAIRY SCHOOL Drop-out** on all her fabulous adventures!